Fear The Bloody Forest In The Dark

Volume 1

By

Samantha

Samantha

Dedication

To those who doubted me... I struggled with English and writing, came from an abusive background, and was silent until I was 6. Born on Halloween, I've achieved my biggest dream, this book. My boyfriend's courage sparked my writing. My mind is my greatest craft.

Acknowledgement

To my partner, who encouraged me to write and publish this book. Thank you for your constant support.

And to Mr john Wesley and Chloe Walter at London Book Publishers

Table of Contents

The Bed That Moved in the Mental Health Ward

I can barely breathe. My nerves are on fire, my mind spiraling with confusion and grief. It's been weeks since my mother, Macy, died, a sudden, brutal end to a life I thought would always anchor mine. The tumor spread so fast the doctors couldn't even promise a goodbye. Now all I feel is an endless, gnawing emptiness inside me.

I haven't slept all night. I lie in bed, staring at the ceiling, wishing the ache would break. By dawn, the walls of my mind feel like they're collapsing inward. I pick up the phone with trembling fingers and call the hospital. I don't even remember what I say. Something about feeling unsafe, about being lost. About needing someone, anyone.

Hours later, I am sitting stiffly in a cold waiting room, my hands knotted tightly in my lap. A psychiatrist eventually calls me in for evaluation. I stumble through answers, barely able to form thoughts, my body hollowed out with exhaustion. After what feels like eternity, he admits me to the mental health ward under a section. Part of me feels relief. Another part screams that I'm more alone now than ever.

They assign me a small room, just a bed bolted to the floor, a tiny TV hanging crookedly on the wall, and a wardrobe with a creaky door. I hang up a few clothes I managed to bring and collapse onto the stiff mattress. The room smells sterile, but underneath there's something else... something sour and old.

My chest tightens. I think of my mother again, of how sudden it all was. One moment she was smiling; the next, she was a whisper fading from this world. A sob bubbles up my throat, but I push it down. I have to survive this.

A nurse brings me a sleeping pill, Nitrazepam, to help me rest. I swallow it without protest. Sleep, that's all I need. Just sleep.

But around 3 a.m., the world tilts.

At first, I think it's a dream. A deep, lucid nightmare. But no, I'm awake, and the bed beneath me is moving. Shaking. Trembling like it's alive.

I try to sit up, but I can't. My body refuses to obey. I'm weightless, no, I'm suspended, the bed rising slowly into the air. A cold sweat breaks across my skin. I open my mouth to scream, but no sound comes out. My voice is trapped inside me, just like the rest of me.

The room is dead silent... until it isn't.

From the walls, whispers begin to echo, ghostly, taunting. They grow louder, morphing into a sinister booing, then laughter. The laughter is sharp and cruel, slithering under my skin.

And then, the blood.

Thick, sticky drops fall from nowhere, splattering against my clothes and skin. I writhe against invisible chains, but I can't move, can't run, can't hide.

The room darkens, shadows pooling in the corners, gathering... forming.

A figure emerges from the gloom.

Not a white, wispy spirit like I'd seen in movies. No, this one is solid. A black ghost, a woman, her face twisted in rage, her eyes pits of endless hate. She glides toward me, silent except for the soft slither of her movement.

She knows my name.

"Amy," she hisses, the sound of it making my blood run cold. "Amyyyy..."

I try to turn away, but the bed jolts, pinning me further. The ghost circles me like a vulture, the air around her vibrating with a malevolent force. I feel invisible blows to my stomach, like fists driving the breath from my body, but there's nothing there except her unblinking gaze.

Hours pass like centuries. Torture after torture. Whispers, touches, blows. I am trapped in a nightmare that has claws.

Samantha

And still, no one comes.

Just as the despair threatens to consume me, there's a knock on the door.

The ghost's head jerks toward the sound. In a blink, she vanishes, sucked away like smoke into the cracks of the walls.

The bed crashes to the floor with a thud that shakes my bones.

I lie sprawled on the ground, shaking, my breath coming in ragged gasps. The nurse opens the door, cheerful and oblivious. But her smile falters when she sees me, sees the blood, the terror carved into my face.

I stammer out the words: "This room... it's haunted. Please... move me."

The nurse hesitates, glancing around the room as if sensing the dark presence still lingering. She nods quickly. I'm moved by the end of the day.

Later, I overhear whispers among the staff. They padlock my old room shut. No one ever sleeps there again. Patients cross themselves when they walk by, quickening their steps past the boarded-up glass door. Behind it, something waits.

I recovered, in time. But deep inside, a part of me knows: the ghost is still there.

Waiting. Watching.

Waiting for the next broken soul to come through her door.

The Earth That Became Black

Halloween had always been my favorite time of year, a night where darkness was expected, even welcomed. But nothing could have prepared me for the darkness that found us that night.

It was October 31st, just after midnight had bled into November 1st, my birthday. The air was cold and sharp, slicing through my jacket as I wandered across the empty fields with my best friend. Our laughter from earlier had died down to whispers, our boots crunching against the frost-coated grass.

The fields stretched out endlessly before us, ghostly and pale under the weak light of the half-moon. The icy ground numbed my feet, each step sending a shiver up my spine. My friend pulled their coat tighter, visibly trembling, though whether from the chill or unease, I couldn't tell.

We shouldn't have been out so late. I realize that now.

The night seemed to grow colder with every breath we took. A strange stillness settled over the field, no wind, no sounds of animals or distant traffic. Just silence so heavy it pressed against my ears.

And then it happened.

Without warning, the sky above us, and the ground beneath our feet, turned black. Not dark the way a cloud covers the moon. Not the soft darkness of a normal night.

Black.

Total, suffocating, endless blackness, as if someone had poured ink across the universe itself.

I froze, heart hammering inside my chest. I could barely see my own hand in front of my face. Around us, an unnatural stickiness filled the air, something thick began to fall from the sky. I wiped my hands across my jacket instinctively, but the sensation only grew worse.

It was sticky... warm... and the smell...

Samantha

I gagged as the metallic scent hit my nose, the unmistakable, stomach-churning stench of blood.

Panic clawed at my throat. My friend whimpered beside me, but the blackness swallowed even the sound, muffling everything except the wet splatters of the blood-like rain.

"What the hell is happening?" I tried to whisper, but my voice was swallowed by the thick, oily air.

Somewhere above us, unseen through the suffocating dark, something stirred.

Something was coming.

The ground beneath us pulsed as if alive, as if it too had been swallowed by whatever had taken the sky.

We staggered backward, slipping on the now greasy, slimy earth. I raised my hands again, wiping at my face, but the substance only smeared thicker across my skin.

It coated everything, the grass, the trees in the distance, the very air we breathed.

The stench grew unbearable. It wasn't just the coppery tang of blood; it was rot, decay, something ancient and foul dredged up from a place no human was ever meant to touch.

I wiped my palms against my jacket, but the sticky liquid clung stubbornly, stringing between my fingers like webbing. It seeped through my clothes, heavy and sickeningly warm.

My friend let out a broken sob, eyes wide and shining in the faint glow of what little light remained.

"This isn't rain," they whispered, voice trembling. "It's... it's not water."

I tried to answer, to say something that would make it all seem logical, explainable. But no words came. Deep down, something primal inside me understood, this was not a storm.

Fear The Bloody Forest In The Dark

This was something else.

Something worse.

Overhead, the darkness shifted, a rolling mass of shadows and sickly, pulsing lights, and for a moment, I swore I saw shapes moving within it. Shapes that didn't belong to anything of this earth.

My heart pounded so hard it hurt.

We were no longer standing on the field where we had laughed and joked just an hour ago.

We were somewhere else now.

Somewhere wrong.

And whatever had turned the earth black... it wasn't done with us yet.

Halloween had always been my favorite time of year, a night where darkness was expected, even welcomed. But nothing could have prepared me for the darkness that found us that night. It was October 31st, just after midnight had bled into November 1st, my birthday. The air was cold and sharp, slicing through my jacket as I wandered across the empty fields with my best friend. Our laughter from earlier had died down to whispers, our boots crunching against the frost-coated grass. The fields stretched out endlessly before us, ghostly and pale under the weak light of the half-moon. The icy ground numbed my feet, each step sending a shiver up my spine. My friend pulled their coat tighter, visibly trembling, though whether from the chill or unease, I couldn't tell.

We shouldn't have been out so late. I realize that now. The night seemed to grow colder with every breath we took. A strange stillness settled over the field, no wind, no sounds of animals or distant traffic. Just silence so heavy it pressed against my ears. And then it happened. Without warning, the sky above us, and the ground beneath our feet, turned black. Not dark the way a cloud covers the moon. Not the soft darkness of a normal night. Black. Total, suffocating, endless blackness, as if someone had poured ink across the universe itself.

I froze, heart hammering inside my chest. I could barely see my own hand in front of my face. Around us, an unnatural stickiness filled the air, something thick began to fall from the sky. I wiped my hands across my jacket instinctively, but the sensation only grew worse. It coated everything, the grass, the trees in the distance, the very air we breathed. The stench grew unbearable. It wasn't just the coppery tang of blood; it was rot, decay, something ancient and foul dredged up from a place no human was ever meant to touch. My friend let out a broken sob, eyes wide and shining in the faint glow of what little light remained. "This isn't rain," they whispered, voice trembling. "It's... it's not water." I tried to answer, to say something that would make it all seem logical, explainable. But no words came. Deep down, something primal inside me understood, this was not a storm. This was something else. Something worse.

The rumble started low, a trembling deep within the earth that made my teeth chatter. At first, I thought it was another part of the nightmare, the sky hemorrhaging blackness, the blood-like rain. But when I looked up, wiping the sticky slime from my eyes, I saw it. Lights. Blazing white and red, cutting through the pitch black. A round, massive object was descending from the sky, its underside pulsing with strange patterns. The air buzzed with electricity, the very molecules around us vibrating like a plucked wire. I grabbed my friend's arm, frozen in place as we stared, helpless. With a deafening hiss, the craft landed in the middle of the field, flattening the tall grass into blackened, smoking circles. A panel slid open along its side with a metallic groan, and a staircase unfolded slowly, almost invitingly.

We should have run. We didn't. Figures emerged from the ship, four of them. Tall, slender, humanoid, but wrong in ways my brain refused to fully process. Their skin glistened in the black rain, their movements sharp and unnatural. Their eyes, black, slanted, shining with a cold, calculating hunger, locked onto us immediately. Two moved in front of us, two behind, cutting off any hope of escape. I turned to run, but it was too late. A hiss of gas burst from their hands, a sweet, cloying smell that filled my nostrils before I could even scream. My legs buckled. The world tilted. Darkness swallowed me whole.

Fear The Bloody Forest In The Dark

I woke to cold metal pressing against my back. Blinking hard, I realized I was lying inside a cavernous room, the ceiling a swirling mass of strange lights and symbols. My friend was next to me, strapped down, eyes fluttering open in a drugged haze. The aliens moved around us, silent and methodical, as if we were nothing more than specimens under a microscope. Terror coursed through me. I struggled against the bonds but they held firm. One of the figures leaned over me, its cold black eyes boring into mine. I tried to speak, tried to plead, but no sound came. Only the wild pounding of my heart filled my ears.

And then the pain began. A searing, wrenching pain in my abdomen, like something inside me was being ripped apart and reassembled at the same time. I screamed silently, arching against the restraints. In mere moments, impossibly fast, a sharp, alien cry pierced the air. I turned my head, sweat and tears blinding me, and saw it. A creature. Small, misshapen, its head large and bulbous, its eyes too black, too deep. It was cradled by one of the aliens, its mouth opening and closing in unnatural, jerky motions. It wasn't human. It wasn't anything I should have been able to create. But somehow, somehow, it was mine. I felt something slip from my body. A pulling, draining sensation, as if my very soul had been yanked out and handed over to them. I wept, not from the physical pain, but from the sheer violation of it all.

The next thing I remember was the cold sting of rain against my face. I lay crumpled on the blood-soaked field, my friend beside me, both of us dazed and broken. The spaceship was gone. The black sky had faded, replaced by the dull gray of early morning. The sticky substance had vanished, leaving only a damp, foul-smelling earth behind. I tried to stand, but my body refused. Every muscle, every bone felt foreign. As if I no longer belonged to myself. Memories flickered in and out of focus, the aliens, the dark room, the creature born from my body. But already the details were slipping away, like a dream you try desperately to hold onto after waking. Had it even happened? A part of me hoped it hadn't. A larger part knew it had.

Samantha

I never spoke about that night. Not to my friend. Not to anyone. Who would believe me? Who could possibly understand the horror of it? The fear rooted itself deep inside me, a constant companion. I became afraid of the sky, afraid of walking across open fields, afraid of the dark. Afraid of myself. And sometimes, even now, I feel a faint flutter inside me, a reminder. A piece of that nightmare still lingering, waiting, hidden under my skin. The Earth turned black once. And deep down, I know it could happen again.

The Snow Monster

Winter had wrapped the world in its cold, unrelenting grip. It was the perfect time for an adventure, or so we thought. A group of us had been craving an escape, a week away into the wild beauty of the snowy mountains, and we finally made it happen. Excitement buzzed between us as we packed the car, layering ourselves in thick coats and winter boots, ready to take on the frozen landscape. The day we set off was bitterly cold; the wind whipped across the roads with a ferocity that made the trees bend and groan. But our spirits were high, and nothing, not even the biting air, was going to ruin our plans.

The drive into the mountains was like stepping into another world. The farther we went, the thicker the snow grew, burying everything in a vast sea of white. Towering pine trees dusted in snow lined the roads, their dark trunks contrasting sharply against the endless whiteness. When we reached the national park, we paused to take it all in, it was breathtaking. The air was sharp in our lungs, and the deep snow crunched loudly beneath our boots as we unloaded the car. Grabbing our camping gear, we headed through the park gates, walking deeper and deeper into the heart of the wilderness. The world was eerily silent around us, broken only by our laughter and the distant howls of the wind.

After what felt like hours of trekking through the thick snow, we found the perfect spot to camp. A clearing surrounded by ancient trees, the ground layered deep with untouched snow. We set up our tents and built a fire, stacking logs into a small, crackling blaze that cast warm sparks into the growing night. The snow continued to fall, light and soft at first, dusting our shoulders and sticking to our hats, but we barely noticed. We brewed tea over the fire, our fingers thawing over the mugs, and for a while, it felt like we were part of something timeless, just us, the mountains, and the falling snow.

But as the hours slipped by, the sky turned a deeper shade of gray, and the snow began to fall harder, faster. The fire struggled against the rising wind, the flames snapping wildly. We decided it was time to call it a night. After dousing the fire, we retreated into our tents, bundled into our sleeping bags, and tried to find warmth against the creeping cold. Outside, the storm grew ferocious, snow piling up around the tents, the wind howling like a chorus of unseen wolves. We turned off the flashlight to conserve its battery, lying in darkness, listening to the storm rage against the thin fabric that separated us from the wild.

It was sometime in the dead of night, maybe just before midnight, when I first heard it, a deep, heavy crunching of snow outside the tent. At first, I thought it was the storm playing tricks on my ears. But then came the low, guttural snuffling, a wet, heavy breath just inches from where I lay. I held my breath, my heart thundering painfully in my chest. A massive shadow loomed against the thin tent wall, towering, hulking. Its movements were deliberate, purposeful. I could hear it sniffing, the sound deep and wet, and then, a roar, low and furious, that shook the very ground beneath us.

We froze, too terrified to speak. Through the thin material, I caught a glimpse of fur, massive paws, and the glint of teeth. It was a grizzly bear, a giant, made monstrous by the storm. It rose up on its hind legs, its full weight pressing against the side of the tent. The fabric strained and then tore as razor-sharp claws slashed through it like paper. Snow and freezing wind rushed in. We scrambled, but there was nowhere to go, no weapons, no ranger station for miles, just a few thin layers of cloth and our own pounding fear.

The bear roared again, louder this time, a sound that rattled inside my bones. Its claws raked the ground inches from where I lay curled, shivering not just from the cold but from pure, primal terror. I could smell its hot, rancid breath. I could hear its snarling, feel the vibrations in the earth as it pawed and tore at our little shelter. We were trapped, utterly helpless against the power of the storm, and the monster it had awakened.

Then, out of nowhere, a blinding light slashed across the sky. It wasn't lightning, it was something else, something unnatural. A long, arcing beam of brilliant white fire, streaking over the mountains, lighting up the whole world for a heartbeat. The bear froze, its snout lifted toward the heavens, a low whine rumbling in its throat. Without warning, it turned and lumbered away, its massive paws leaving deep, ragged tracks in the snow that quickly began to fill with fresh powder.

We lay there for a long time, too afraid to move, listening to the silence that followed. Eventually, when the first gray light of dawn began to seep through the storm clouds, we crawled from what was left of our tent. The snow was knee-deep, the camp in ruins, but we were alive. We followed the trail of paw prints a short distance, watching as they vanished into the endless white. Whatever that light had been, comet, flare, something beyond our understanding, it had saved us.

We packed up what little we had left and made our way back toward the car, our breath fogging in the icy morning air. The mountains, so beautiful and serene when we arrived, now seemed to loom over us, cold and indifferent. We didn't speak much on the way down. What was there to say? We had looked death in the face in that frozen wilderness, and only by some miracle, or something far stranger, had we survived.

It was supposed to be a fun winter holiday. Instead, it became a nightmarish memory, frozen forever beneath the snow.

Baghead Killer One-Eye Monster

The night was bitter cold, the kind that seeped through walls and windows, gnawed at your bones, and made even the deepest corners of the house feel hollow. Darkness clung to everything outside my window, an endless black that pressed against the glass. I should have been sleeping, wrapped in blankets, trying to ignore the chill, but I wasn't. Something gnawed at me from within, something born from the nightmare I had just woken from.

It wasn't just any dream. It was one I had been having over and over, a man, tall and broad, with a filthy potato sack pulled over his head. Only one eye showed through a rough, jagged hole, glinting with pure malice. In the dream, he carried a machete, its silver blade flashing in the darkness. I woke gasping, drenched in cold sweat, my heart thudding painfully against my ribs. This dream wasn't just a dream anymore. I could feel it, deep down, it was a warning.

Trembling, I grabbed my phone and called my friends, Shandy, Bex, and Oscar. I needed them. I couldn't explain why, not fully, but they came without question, showing up at my door within minutes. We bundled ourselves in thick clothes, pulled boots over our feet, grabbed a flashlight, and headed into the night. It was close to 2 a.m. when we set off, our breath clouding the air, boots crunching over the frozen ground. I didn't know if what I saw was real or just fear gripping my mind, but I had to find out.

The woods loomed ahead of us, the old gate creaking on its hinges as we pushed it open. The trees groaned and swayed under the cold wind, branches scratching at each other like skeletal fingers. Leaves, wet and sticky, clung to the muddy path. I nearly slipped once but caught myself before falling. We pressed on, deeper into the woods, our flashlight cutting a narrow beam of pale light through the darkness. Above us, the sky was a blank void, no stars, no moon, just blackness. The world felt muted, like we had stepped into another realm.

I tried to shake off the fear clinging to me, but it was no use. Every green bush, every whisper of wind against the branches made my skin crawl. Then I felt it, a tap on my shoulder. I spun around fast, the beam of the flashlight shaking wildly in my hand. My breath froze in my throat.

Standing not ten feet away was the figure from my nightmare.

The baghead man. The single gleaming eye. The blood-stained machete dangling from his hand.

For one awful moment, the world stopped. Then instinct took over, I turned and ran, not daring to look back. Trees blurred past me, the cold air tearing at my face. I screamed for Shandy, for Bex, for Oscar, but there was no answer. No footsteps behind me, no shouts. I was alone.

Terror clawed at my throat. I ran blindly, crashing through underbrush, slipping in the mud. Somehow, through the chaos, I spotted the faint outline of the gate up ahead. Salvation. I pushed myself harder, ignoring the burning in my legs, the freezing air stabbing at my lungs.

And then I saw them.

Hanging from the trees.

Their bodies, my friends, strung up like grotesque ornaments. Blood dripped from their limbs, soaking into the damp leaves below. I stumbled backward, a raw scream tearing from my throat. Tears blurred my vision.,. My heart shattered into a thousand pieces. I had brought them here. I had killed them.

Movement in the corner of my eye, I turned to see the Baghead killer advancing, machete swinging lazily at his side. He didn't rush. He didn't have to. He knew he had me.

I bolted for the gate, slipping and sliding through the muck. My hands hit the cold iron, and I pushed myself through with everything I had. Behind me, I heard a roar of anger, but I didn't look back. I didn't dare. I ran and ran until the woods were only a shadow behind me.

Somehow, I made it home.

I locked the doors, pulled the curtains tight, and collapsed onto the floor, sobbing. Hours later, numb and shaking, I turned on the TV, expecting, praying, to see something. Missing persons reports. News alerts. But there was nothing. No mention of Shandy, Bex, or Oscar. As if they had never existed.

I never spoke about that night. I told no one about the horrors that lurked in the woods. I buried it deep inside, pretending it was just a nightmare, even though I knew the truth. The Baghead One eye killer was still out there, hiding in the blood-curdling darkness, waiting for his next victim. And the worst part?

Somewhere deep down, I knew he would find one.

The Train That Drinks Blood

It was the dead of winter, and I stood alone on the icy platform of the railway station. Snow fell in thick, relentless waves, the sky a heavy, lifeless grey. I shivered, teeth chattering, despite the thick coat wrapped tightly around me and the insulated boots on my feet. The station was deserted, unsurprising, since it was only 6 a.m.

I was beginning a long journey, traveling from India to the far north of Pakistan. The cold was brutal, the kind that numbed fingers and slowed thought, and I welcomed the warmth of the train when it pulled in on time, its headlights barely cutting through the falling snow.

The train hissed as it came to a stop. The doors opened with a metallic sigh, but barely anyone got off. It felt odd, but not frightening. In fact, I was grateful. A quiet train meant a peaceful ride. No crowds, no noise, no pushing. Just me and the journey.

I stepped inside, found a cabin with sleeping berths, and settled into one. The restaurant car offered only a limited menu, some hot drinks, tea, coffee, a few snacks, but it was enough.

The departure was smooth. At precisely 6:45, the train doors sealed shut, and the engine rumbled to life. As we rolled forward into the snowstorm, I settled into the berth, took out a novel, and began to read. Hours slipped by. The world outside the windows turned into a shifting blur of white, the blizzard intensifying with every mile.

As darkness fell, the sense of calm began to erode. Something was off.

I realized I hadn't seen or heard a single person since the train began moving. No conductors, no announcements, no footsteps in the hallway. The compartments I passed earlier had all appeared empty, but I had assumed the other passengers were simply asleep. Now, that assumption felt fragile.

Curious, and uneasy, I decided to walk the length of the train. Car after car passed beneath my feet. Every seat was vacant. Every berth unoccupied. There were no voices, no movement, nothing but the hum of the train and the soft groan of the wind outside.

Samantha

Then I stepped in something.

It was wet and warm, and it clung to the sole of my boot with a sickening stickiness. I looked down, and my heart lurched.

Blood.

A dark crimson trail streaked across the floor and smeared along the wall, as though something had been dragged through the corridor. It was fresh. Still glistening.

My breath caught in my throat. I turned quickly and hurried toward the front of the train. My only thought was to reach the control cabin, to find the conductor, to make sense of this madness.

When I arrived, I knocked hard on the cabin door.

No answer.

I knocked again. Louder.

Still nothing.

I twisted the handle. Locked.

Through the small glass window, I saw only shadows. No lights. No movement. No one was there.

The train was moving.

But no one was driving it.

Panic began to set in. I tried the emergency stop panel, it was dead. I pushed every button I could find, every lever, every control. None responded. I ran to the nearest exit and tried the side doors, but they wouldn't budge. They were sealed shut as though welded from the outside.

I was trapped.

A cold sweat broke over my skin despite the heat. The train was in motion, but there was no conductor, no passengers, and no way out. Just me, and the trail of blood.

Fear The Bloody Forest In The Dark

I returned to my berth and sat down, heart pounding in my chest. I couldn't shake the sense of dread curling around me. I hadn't imagined the blood. I hadn't imagined the silence. Something terrible had happened on this train.

Then I heard it.

A sound from the front of the train, deep and guttural. Not mechanical. Not natural. It was a gurgling noise, like a machine choking, or a throat being cleared... with something thick.

I knew I shouldn't go back. But I had to.

I moved quietly through the carriages, following the sound until I reached the engine room. The door creaked open with a long, whining groan.

Inside, I nearly vomited.

The walls were smeared with blood. The metal floor was slick with it, pooling around the base of the massive engine. Pipes dripped crimson. The air was thick with the coppery scent of death.

And in the center of it all... something moved.

A shadow.

It was massive, covered in matted, dark fur, hunched over the engine like a beast feeding. Its hands, long, clawed, inhuman, gripped a heavy container. It tipped the container into the open mouth of the engine, and thick red liquid spilled inside.

Blood.

The engine sizzled and roared to life with new energy, drinking deeply. The creature turned slightly, and I saw the glint of its eyes, yellow, wild, aware.

I backed away slowly, trying not to breathe, trying not to be heard.

This train didn't run on fuel.

It ran on blood.

I stumbled back to my cabin, hands shaking. My thoughts spiraled.

Samantha

Where were the passengers?

I had seen them get off... but none had boarded with me. None had appeared in the corridors. Not even one.

Had they ever been there?

Or had they... already been fed to the engine?

I didn't know why I was still alive. But I knew I wouldn't be for long if I didn't find a way off. The train showed no signs of stopping. No stations. No roads. Nothing but endless white outside the windows.

I was alone.

On a train that fed on the dead.

And the worst part? Morning was approaching. But I was still locked inside.

With it.

Early evening in the summer time

It was early evening, and the air still held the warmth of a long summer day. The sun dipped low in the sky, casting golden light through our kitchen window as I sat finishing my meal with Wesley, my closest friend and partner in nearly everything. We were laughing over something trivial when the conversation drifted to the idea of an adventure, just a few days away from everything, camping out in the forest that bordered our town in Utah. We had no pets to worry about, no children tugging at our sleeves, and no real responsibilities that weekend. The timing felt perfect.

"My name's Kelly," I remember saying aloud, as if it would help make the decision feel more real. "And I think it's going to be a beautiful weekend."

Wesley grinned, and together we cleared the table, washed the dishes, and talked about the supplies we'd need. The week passed quickly, filled with anticipation. By Friday, we had packed our tent, sleeping bags, cookware, and basic gear. Food, we planned to grab on the way. We were giddy, like two kids sneaking off to play in the woods. It felt spontaneous and free.

We drove with the windows down, music playing low, the mountains rising around us like sleeping giants. When we arrived, the small dirt carpark near the forest entrance was empty. Perfect. We slipped on our hiking boots, hoisted our gear onto our backs, and opened the wooden gate at the trailhead.

The forest swallowed us almost immediately.

The path was long and winding, lined with towering pine trees so dense we could barely see the sky. The air inside was cooler, shaded, and filled with the earthy scent of needles and bark. As we walked deeper, the light grew dim and the silence thickened. The only sounds were the crunch of gravel under our boots and the occasional whistle of wind rustling through the treetops.

Still, it wasn't unsettling. Not yet.

Samantha

We hiked a good distance in before settling on a spot just off the trail, flat, quiet, surrounded by trees. Together, we pitched the tent, gathered fallen branches for a fire, and made a plan to find water before dark. We had flashlights and a penknife, and neither of us felt nervous. After all, we were just two people enjoying a weekend in nature.

But as we wandered farther in search of a stream, something began to shift.

The path curved downward into a steep slope, and the trees pressed closer together. The forest floor grew uneven, and our boots slid slightly on loose stones. That was when I tripped.

Pain shot up my leg, and I crumpled to the ground, clutching my ankle. "Sprained," I hissed.

Wesley knelt beside me, concerned, but after resting a bit, I was able to limp forward. The pain dulled, manageable for now. We pressed on, hoping to find water before nightfall.

The sky above had deepened to indigo. Through cracks in the canopy, stars began to blink into view, and the full moon cast a silver glow across the forest floor. It should have been beautiful.

But then... we heard it.

Voices.

Low, rhythmic chanting. Not in English. Not in any language I recognized. It wasn't coming from ahead or behind, it seemed to vibrate from the trees themselves. My blood turned to ice.

"It's probably just a group of hikers messing around," Wesley whispered.

But we both knew it wasn't.

The sound grew louder, closer. It felt wrong, like a horror film soundtrack bleeding into real life. Then came the footsteps. Before we could react, hands grabbed us from behind.

We screamed, fought, kicked, but they were too strong.

Fear The Bloody Forest In The Dark

They dragged us through the trees to a clearing hidden deep in the woods. It was marked by a massive symbol scorched into the earth, a star enclosed in a circle, blackened and smoking faintly at the edges. Torches stood at each point, flickering like tongues of fire in the darkness.

And in the center of the star... stood him.

The devil, or something close enough to it.

He was grotesque, towering, with leathery skin, wild eyes that glowed red in the firelight, and sharp, uneven teeth that clacked as he muttered spells in a voice like gravel dragged over metal. A thick ring pierced his nose. His presence alone was paralyzing.

Wesley and I were tied to separate trees, our arms bound tightly behind our backs. I was too terrified to speak. Too frozen to move. The devil began pacing around the star, chanting in a guttural language, while robed figures emerged from the darkness, humanoid, yes, but dressed like monks twisted by nightmare. Their faces were hidden behind black and white masks, featureless but watching.

Then everything went black.

I fainted.

When I came to, the fire was still burning, and the devil's face hovered inches from mine, his breath hot and sour against my skin. I tried to scream, but my voice caught in my throat. Wesley was gagged and barely conscious. The cultists circled the star, chanting louder now, wild and feverish.

The devil raised his hands to the sky and cried out. I couldn't understand his words, but I felt their meaning in my bones. He didn't want our lives.

He wanted a child.

His child.

A devil baby, born from a human womb, created not through love or science, but dark magic. He needed a soul to anchor the spell, and I was the chosen vessel.

He lifted me from the ground and hooked my body onto a twisted iron pole at the center of the ritual. Symbols burned into the ground beneath me. I couldn't scream. I couldn't move. My limbs were heavy, my thoughts scattered. I was half-awake, half-dreaming.

But then, I remembered.

The penknife.

In a flash of desperation, I shifted just enough to reach it in my pocket. My fingers worked the blade open, and I sawed frantically at the rope until it snapped. My hands free, I grabbed a fire starter from the devil's altar, something one of the cultists had carelessly left behind.

I lit the edge of the ritual circle.

The fire caught instantly.

Flames roared through the star, consuming the symbols and shooting high into the sky. The robed figures screamed, stumbling backward. The devil howled, a sound so loud and horrible it shook the trees. His body writhed in the center of the blaze, black smoke pouring from his mouth as he screamed:

"I'll be back for you two! My child lives in you! My curse will follow your soul!"

I grabbed Wesley, cut his ropes, and we ran.

We didn't stop.

Not when we reached the tent, not when we threw our gear into the trunk, not even when we peeled out of the carpark, tires skidding on the gravel. We screamed. We cried. We didn't speak a word for the entire drive home.

Three days later, I knew it was true.

I was pregnant.

Fear The Bloody Forest In The Dark

Not by Wesley. Not by any human means.

Something had taken root inside me, something dark.

I did not keep the child.

But I never went near the forest again.

Samantha

The Hole in the Tunnel

The summer evening hung heavy with heat, the kind that lingers even as the sun begins to dip low in the sky. The air was thick and still, the streets nearly silent. It was the kind of Saturday that crawls, slow and sleepy, until the world finally exhales.

I was in the kitchen, wiping sweat from my forehead as I pulled a roast chicken from the oven. Not exactly a meal for a scorching summer night, but cravings are cravings. Roast potatoes, seasoned to perfection, completed the plate. And no, before anyone asks, I was not pregnant. I am well into my fifties. Just had a fierce appetite that day and no one around to question it.

My best friend Sally had joined me for dinner, as she often did. We had known each other for decades. She had a family of her own, grown now, but we still carved out time for these little rituals. Laughs over the table, shared memories, stories we've told too many times but still laugh at anyway.

We didn't bother with dessert, though we did treat ourselves to a couple of ice cream bars from the freezer. After we'd eaten and washed up, we both leaned back on the couch, rubbing our stomachs and joking about how full we were.

But instead of slipping into a lazy night in, we did something different.

"We need to walk this off," Sally said, patting her belly.

I agreed. The heat had finally begun to ease, the sky a warm orange fading into indigo. We grabbed our shoes and headed out toward the trail that looped around the edge of the forest.

The light was soft and golden as we wandered past wild grass and tall trees. That was when we saw it.

At the edge of the forest, hidden behind some overgrown bushes, was a massive hole in the earth. Covered in shadows and thick with branches, it didn't look natural. We pushed the greenery aside, and gasped.

Fear The Bloody Forest In The Dark

It wasn't a hole.

It was an old train tunnel.

Long-abandoned, the mouth of it yawned open like some dark, waiting mouth. A heavy silence hung around it, broken only by the distant hum of cicadas. Neither of us had ever seen it before, despite living here for years.

"We should check it out," I said.

Sally hesitated. "We don't have a flashlight."

"So? Let's just go in a little. See how far we can get."

"My name's Megan," I added with a grin, "and I am not about to let a little tunnel scare me."

So, we stepped inside.

It was instantly colder, cool, damp air rising from the stone floor. Our eyes adjusted slowly to the dark as we walked, our footsteps echoing off the tunnel walls. Dust and gravel crunched beneath our shoes. Bits of old track stuck out in rusted, twisted lines.

About twenty feet in, the light behind us had all but vanished. We could still see each other, but barely.

Sally's voice broke the silence. "Megan... do you hear that?"

I paused. A faint sound, rattling, dry and sharp, echoed from deeper in the tunnel. It wasn't metal. It wasn't wind.

Something was moving.

We both froze. The noise grew louder.

Then, out of the darkness, something slithered past us.

It moved with speed, too fast to register. But what we *did* see was unmistakable: scales. A wide, flat head. A tail that shook violently, the rattle deafening in the echoing space.

A rattlesnake.

And not just one.

Another slid out behind it, then another. Within seconds, we were surrounded. A whole nest, maybe dozens, had made this tunnel home. We had wandered straight into their den.

"Oh my God," Sally whispered, her voice trembling.

I couldn't speak. I was paralyzed.

One of them struck.

Sally screamed, dropping to the ground, clutching her leg. Another bite, then another. She was hit multiple times. Her skin turned pale as sweat broke out across her forehead. I could see her trembling.

I had to do something.

My heart was pounding, my hands shaking, but I remembered something from a survival article I'd read. I ripped off my shirt, tearing it into strips, and tied them tightly above the bite marks to slow the venom's spread. I didn't care about the cold, I had to help her.

"We'll get out," I said, though I wasn't sure I believed it. "Just hold on."

One of the snakes backed off.

Then another.

Seizing the moment, I grabbed Sally's arm and pulled her to her feet. We moved fast, half-carrying, half-running, out of the tunnel. The snakes hissed behind us, but they didn't follow. Maybe they'd done enough.

Back in the open air, I held her up as we stumbled down the trail. Her face was gray, her breaths shallow. I didn't have a phone. We had to find someone. Anyone.

At the edge of the forest, near the old gate, I saw a man, just a silhouette in the fading light.

I screamed.

"Help! Please! My friend's been bitten!"

He ran toward us and caught Sally as she collapsed into his arms. Without hesitation, he helped carry her to his car. We drove to the hospital at breakneck speed. It wasn't far, but every second felt like forever.

We got there just in time.

They rushed her inside, hooked her to IVs, monitored her heartbeat. She was barely conscious but alive.

I sat in the waiting room for hours. I couldn't leave, not until I knew. I called her family. I paced. I prayed.

The call came late that night.

"She's stable," the nurse said. "She'll be here a few days, but she's going to make it."

I sank into the chair and cried.

A week later, Sally came home. We still laugh, nervously, about that night. About how a simple walk turned into a nightmare.

We don't take that trail anymore.

We don't joke about exploring tunnels, either.

Because the hole in the tunnel was more than just a relic of the past.

It was a home for something deadly, and for one summer night, it became our hell.

Ice Cream

Summer had finally arrived. It was one of those brilliant, golden mornings where the sun seemed to split the flags on the pavement, and the trees stood still under a warm blue sky. The flowers looked brighter than usual, soaking in the sun. A perfect day.

I got dressed, made a quick breakfast, and decided to head out for some shopping. I had a craving for new spring clothes, pastel shades, light fabrics, and maybe a pair of sandals. I called my good friend George. We weren't a couple, just close. I was Lily Mae, he was George, and we were both in our early forties with no kids and no family to tie us down. We liked our freedom and our peace.

We met at 11 a.m. on that sunny Saturday. I went to his place first, he lived alone, like me. As we walked through the shops, bright displays of bags, shoes, and fresh styles caught our eyes. But something else pulled us in unexpectedly: a last-minute travel deal plastered on the window of a local travel agency.

A two-week holiday to the Spanish island of Gran Canaria.

The deal was too good to ignore, someone had canceled, and the price had dropped. We looked at each other, both smiling. "Let's do it," George said.

We sat down with the travel agent, flipping through brochures, imagining ourselves under that sun. And before we knew it, we were booked. Our flight left Monday morning.

Excitement buzzed through us. We had the weekend to pack and prep. Since the flight was early, 8 a.m., George stayed at my place Sunday night. It was easier that way.

We were up by 3:30 a.m. that Monday, sleepy but laughing, showering in turns while the taxi waited outside in the wet darkness. The ride to the airport wasn't long. By 5 a.m., the check-in desks were opening. We dropped off our bags, got our boarding passes, and strolled to security.

After clearing the gates, we treated ourselves to a full English breakfast and a pot of tea. We browsed the duty-free shops, George picked out aftershave, I grabbed a lovely perfume. Neither of us smoked or drank much, so we skipped the booze.

Soon, the announcement came for our flight.

We boarded a modest-sized Spanish airline. I got the window seat. As the plane rolled down the runway, the engines roared louder, and then, we were airborne. My first time on a plane, and I loved every second. The clouds stretched below us like soft pillows, and the morning sun gleamed across the sky.

We were served tea and snacks during the flight. It wasn't long before we landed in Gran Canaria, stepping off into a burst of warm, fragrant air.

We collected our suitcases, passed through customs, and took a taxi to our hotel, a charming four-star with a big outdoor pool. The check-in was smooth, and the room was clean and breezy. We went for a swim straight away, the water a welcome break from the heat.

Later, we changed and walked into town for a beautiful outdoor dinner. The days passed gently, sunbathing, exploring, dipping in the pool. By the fifth day, I had a craving for ice cream.

We found a small, colorful parlour just off the beach. The flavors were endless. I chose banana, strawberry, and coconut, topped with syrup, flakes, and served in a chilled tub. George went for peanut butter, bubble gum, and banana. We laughed like teenagers.

Then everything changed.

A man, Spanish, mid-30s, appeared out of nowhere, waving a large knife. His face was twisted, wild, lost in some hallucination. He wasn't drunk, just...gone. Detached from reality.

At first, no one moved. It was like everyone froze in confusion. Then he started screaming, nonsense, fury, and began slashing. People screamed. Three were stabbed before the police arrived.

Samantha

I couldn't breathe. I felt paralyzed. We were trapped at the outdoor tables, ice cream melting in our hands, watching horror unfold. Blood on the pavement, panic all around.

The police ordered him to drop the weapon. He refused.

They had no choice.

They shot him.

He collapsed. The crowd stared, silent, numb. Blood stained the stone walkways, seeping toward the gutter. The ice cream parlour was shut down immediately for a full investigation.

George was calm, steady in a way that grounded me, but I was shaking. Terrified. We headed back to the hotel, trying to make sense of what had just happened. We still had another week of holiday left, but everything felt different.

We stayed, yes. But we were cautious. We avoided crowds, watched every face. I couldn't relax. Couldn't sleep properly. That image of the man, the blade, the screams, it stuck with me.

The trip home came too slowly. I was never so ready to leave a paradise.

Even now, I sometimes flinch when someone walks too close. And I've never looked at an ice cream parlour quite the same way again.

Floating Above the Bed

It had been a long, draining day. The kind of day that wraps itself around your bones and doesn't let go. I'd been on my feet since early morning, deep in spring cleaning mode, moving through the house like a storm. Dusting shelves, scrubbing tiles, dragging the vacuum through every room with mechanical determination. My arms ached, my back screamed, but I was driven by something more than just neatness. Family was coming to stay, and I wanted everything to be perfect. I imagined their smiles, the warmth of conversation, the way the house would hum with life again after being still for so long. That thought kept me going, even when exhaustion tried to slow me down.

By mid-afternoon, with the sun high outside and the house gleaming around me, I decided I deserved a break. A real one. I ran a hot bath, watching the water swirl into the tub, pouring in a ridiculous amount of bubble bath just because it made me happy. The steam curled around my face, the lavender scent rising thick in the air, and I sank beneath the foam with a sigh that came from somewhere deep. It was the kind of bath that untangles muscles and quiets thoughts. I didn't think about anything except how good the heat felt. I stayed in until the water began to cool and my fingers wrinkled like paper.

After toweling off, I pulled on soft nightwear, the fabric cool against my warm skin, and crawled into bed even though the sun was still shining outside. I didn't care. The sheets were fresh, the room still carried the scent of cleaning spray and soap, and for the first time in hours, I felt like I could breathe. I pulled the blanket around me, nestled into the pillow, and closed my eyes. It wasn't supposed to be a long nap, just enough to feel human again. But the moment I shut my eyes, sleep swallowed me whole. Not drifting, not easing. It took me instantly, and I disappeared.

When I opened my eyes again, the room had changed. The golden light of afternoon was gone, replaced by a gray stillness that pressed against the windows. My digital clock glowed faintly: 8:02 PM. I blinked slowly, trying to shake off the fog of sleep, but something felt wrong. Deeply, horribly wrong. I wasn't lying on the bed anymore.

I was above it.

Floating.

My body was suspended in the air, arms and legs dangling like a broken doll. I tried to move, to sit up, to scream, but nothing worked. My limbs were frozen, my mouth sealed shut except for a shallow breath that barely made a sound. Panic erupted inside me, wild and immediate, but I was trapped in silence. My body didn't belong to me. It was like I had been yanked from reality and placed into some otherworldly freeze, a half-life between waking and sleeping.

The room around me was quiet. Too quiet. Not peaceful, oppressive. The air felt thick, unmoving. The kind of quiet that fills your ears and makes your thoughts feel loud. I looked toward the window, searching for something to anchor me back to normal, and that's when I saw the curtains moving. At first, just a gentle sway, as if stirred by a breeze. But the windows were shut. Locked. There was no draft. The air shouldn't have been moving at all.

Then I saw it.

A shadow. A shape. Just past the foot of the bed, standing near the edge of the room where the wall dipped into darkness. At first, it looked like a figure blurred in fog, but the longer I stared, the more solid it became. Not moving. Not speaking. Just watching. And even though it made no sound, I could feel it. The weight of its presence pressed against my chest like something sitting on top of me. My heart pounded, but my body wouldn't respond.

Then it touched me.

I didn't see it move. I only felt it. Cold fingers brushing along my side, tracing over the fabric of my nightwear. The sensation was slow, deliberate, heavy. I wanted to scream, to thrash, to run, but I was still floating, still frozen in mid-air, like I was pinned by some invisible force.

And then, without warning, it stepped forward into the faint light. What I saw shouldn't exist. Its skin was the color of ash, stretched tight over bone, and its mouth was filled with sharp, wet teeth that didn't fit its jaw. Its eyes glowed red, not with light, but with heat, burning like dying coals. Its tongue slithered from between its teeth, impossibly long, and its voice... God, its voice. It wasn't human. It was a rasping, guttural sound, like metal dragged across stone. No words I understood, but the meaning was clear. It was hungry. And it had chosen me.

I watched, paralyzed, as it leaned closer. Horns curved from its skull, twisted and black, and its body pulsed with a kind of energy I couldn't explain. This wasn't a ghost. This was something older. Darker. A demon, real and alive, and it had climbed out of some hidden place to find me.

Time collapsed. I don't know how long I was suspended like that. It felt like hours. The air grew heavier, my skin slick with sweat, and all I could do was hope that it would end. But it didn't. It whispered to me in that inhuman voice, its claws tracing over my body while I floated helplessly. Then I felt something warm and wet below me. I didn't want to look. I didn't want to know. But I knew.

It had done more than touch me.

It had taken something from me.

Left something behind.

I could feel it inside me, like a sickness that hadn't started yet. A weight, low in my stomach, growing heavier with every breath. My hair floated above me like I was underwater, and my skin felt like it was stretched too tight. The demon hovered for a moment longer, staring at me with eyes that had no end, and then it was gone. Not with a scream, not with a blast of smoke, just gone. Pulled back into the shadows it came from.

I dropped.

My body slammed into the mattress, the air punched from my lungs. The room was silent again. The curtains were still. The shape had vanished. But the feeling remained.

Something had changed.

I pulled the blanket around me and lay there, shaking, afraid to sleep, afraid to close my eyes. My body was mine again, but it didn't feel like it. My bed was still there, but it wasn't safe. Something had been in my room that night. Something that didn't belong to this world. And part of it, whatever it was, had stayed behind.

My body was suspended in the air, arms and legs dangling like a broken doll. I tried to move, to sit up, to scream, but nothing worked. My limbs were frozen, my mouth sealed shut except for a shallow breath that barely made a sound. Panic erupted inside me, wild and immediate, but I was trapped in silence. My body didn't belong to me. It was like I had been yanked from reality and placed into some otherworldly freeze, a half-life between waking and sleeping.

The room around me was quiet. Too quiet. Not peaceful, oppressive. The air felt thick, unmoving. The kind of quiet that fills your ears and makes your thoughts feel loud. I looked toward the window, searching for something to anchor me back to normal, and that's when I saw the curtains moving. At first, just a gentle sway, as if stirred by a breeze. But the windows were shut. Locked. There was no draft. The air shouldn't have been moving at all.

Then I saw it.

A shadow. A shape. Just past the foot of the bed, standing near the edge of the room where the wall dipped into darkness. At first, it looked like a figure blurred in fog, but the longer I stared, the more solid it became. Not moving. Not speaking. Just watching. And even though it made no sound, I could feel it. The weight of its presence pressed against my chest like something sitting on top of me. My heart pounded, but my body wouldn't respond.

Then it touched me.

I didn't see it move. I only felt it. Cold fingers brushing along my side, tracing over the fabric of my nightwear. The sensation was slow, deliberate, heavy. I wanted to scream, to thrash, to run, but I was still floating, still frozen in mid-air, like I was pinned by some invisible force.

And then, without warning, it stepped forward into the faint light. What I saw shouldn't exist. Its skin was the color of ash, stretched tight over bone, and its mouth was filled with sharp, wet teeth that didn't fit its jaw. Its eyes glowed red, not with light, but with heat, burning like dying coals. Its tongue slithered from between its teeth, impossibly long, and its voice... God, its voice. It wasn't human. It was a rasping, guttural sound, like metal dragged across stone. No words I understood, but the meaning was clear. It was hungry. And it had chosen me.

I watched, paralyzed, as it leaned closer. Horns curved from its skull, twisted and black, and its body pulsed with a kind of energy I couldn't explain. This wasn't a ghost. This was something older. Darker. A demon, real and alive, and it had climbed out of some hidden place to find me.

Time collapsed. I don't know how long I was suspended like that. It felt like hours. The air grew heavier, my skin slick with sweat, and all I could do was hope that it would end. But it didn't. It whispered to me in that inhuman voice, its claws tracing over my body while I floated helplessly. Then I felt something warm and wet below me. I didn't want to look. I didn't want to know. But I knew.

My night peace had turned into a living hell, a silent torment that stretched beyond the edge of my bed and into something deeper, darker. I wasn't just being haunted, I was being *kept*. My home was no longer mine. It had become a den for something unspeakable. A night demon. A thing made of rage and hunger and possession. It wasn't just touching me anymore, it had *claimed* me. I wasn't just paralyzed. I was *possessed* by something ancient and foul. There were spirits in the room. In the dark of the night, they surrounded me, but the one that pinned me, he was the worst.

Samantha

He held my body in the air, still, suspended, unmoving. I could feel the pressure increasing. His presence grew heavier with each breath I couldn't take. I was alone, truly alone, afraid and motionless, unable to scream, unable to cry. Floating in the air, watching my own fear take shape.

Then I felt it.

The wetness.

A patch of something warm and thick beneath me, clinging to my body in a way that made my skin crawl. It wasn't sweat. It wasn't bathwater. It was something else. Something worse. Something I couldn't unfeel.

It was demon semen.

The words echoed through my head like a curse.

The demon had come not just to terrify me, but to rape me. To torture me. To claim something deeper than flesh. My soul, torn apart under its weight, felt split and branded.

And I still couldn't move.

Even as I looked into the eyes of that red-faced, horned demon, burning with hate and power, I knew I would never be the same. He left me with more than fear. He left me with something growing inside me.

A demon pregnancy.

Hotel Killer Rampage

It was meant to be the trip of a lifetime. A summer escape. A two-week vacation drenched in sunlight, peace, and the kind of quiet you can only find when you're far from home. I had planned everything perfectly, a break abroad, somewhere warm and beautiful, a paradise by the sea. The kind of place where time slows down and your soul exhales. I'd worked hard for it, earned it, and when the day finally arrived, I was buzzing with anticipation. I woke up early that morning, the air already carrying the promise of warmth. I dressed simply, shorts, a loose top, a cardigan draped over my shoulders, and grabbed my suitcase, the wheels bumping against the pavement as I made my way to the waiting taxi. My heart fluttered with excitement. This was it. My time. My break from the world.

The airport was busy, bodies moving in every direction, the mechanical voice of announcements echoing above the crowds. I checked in quickly, slid through security, and found myself a seat in the departure lounge. My bag rested by my feet as I sipped a lukewarm coffee and nibbled on a dry sandwich. Still, none of that mattered. My mind was already somewhere else, drifting along golden beaches, toes buried in hot sand, a drink in hand. The screen above me flickered with the final boarding call, and I stood, stretching, grabbing my things. The plane was nearly full when I boarded, a low hum of conversation all around me, but I found a window seat and settled in. The cabin was cool, sterile, comforting. The seatbelt clicked across my waist, and the engine growled beneath my feet. As we lifted into the sky, I leaned back and smiled, the clouds stretching endlessly below. Hours passed in a haze of sleep and quiet thoughts. Until finally, the captain's voice returned, announcing our descent into paradise.

The air hit me the moment I stepped outside. Hot, thick, and sweet with salt and dust. The sun burned high above, and for a second, everything was perfect. I collected my suitcase, found a taxi, and gave the driver the address of my hotel. We sped along sun-baked roads, palm trees casting long shadows across the pavement. But as we pulled up to the building, the fantasy cracked.

Samantha

It wasn't the shining, modern resort I'd seen in the glossy brochure. It was older, much older. The sign above the door was faded, the paint cracked and peeling. The windows were streaked, the front steps chipped and leaning. My heart dropped, an uncomfortable tightness wrapping around my ribs. Still, I told myself it was fine. Brochures lie. Photos are touched up. I was here now. I had to make the best of it.

Inside, the air was stale. The lobby was dim, the lights flickering overhead, casting long shadows across the tiled floor. The man at the front desk looked up slowly, his eyes dull, uninterested. He handed me the key without a word, the cold metal clinking in my palm. I nodded stiffly and made my way to the elevator. It groaned as it climbed, each floor ticking past like a countdown I didn't understand. My room was small, plain, with old furniture and floral wallpaper curling at the edges. The air conditioner rattled with every breath it took. I stood in the doorway for a moment, wondering what I had just walked into. But I was tired. I needed a shower.

The bathroom tiles were yellowed, the mirror fogged and streaked. The water pressure was weak, the temperature fluctuating, but I stood under it anyway, letting the heat loosen the tension in my back. Afterward, I changed into something light and stepped out into the late afternoon sun, walking to the nearby beach. The ocean was beautiful, blue and endless, and for a few hours, I let myself believe this trip could still be what I had imagined. The wind was soft, the waves calm. But that peace didn't last.

As night fell, I returned to the hotel, the corridors darker now, quieter. The walls seemed closer, the silence more pointed. I ordered room service, just something small, and soon there was a knock at the door. But something about it was off. It was too slow. Too deliberate. The kind of knock that makes your skin tighten.

When I opened the door, a man stood there holding my tray. He was tall, unnervingly so, with a bald head and a long, crooked nose. His eyes were small and too far apart, his hands large and strangely swollen, the nails dark. His shirt was stained, mismatched with his trousers, and his shoes were old, the leather cracked and splitting. He didn't smile. Didn't speak. Just handed me the tray and turned away, his footsteps soft and strange.

I shut the door quickly, locking it. I ate in silence, my appetite dulled by unease. Something wasn't right. I could feel it crawling across my skin. After reading a little to distract myself, I turned out the light and slipped into bed, hoping that sleep would erase the discomfort.

But sometime deep in the night, I woke up to a scream.

It sliced through the silence like glass. I sat up, heart hammering. It was close, inside the building. Then came another sound. A knock. But this time, it was coming from beneath me. From under the floorboards. Slow. Hollow. Rhythmic.

I froze.

My breath caught. I couldn't move. The room felt smaller, the air heavy. I reached for the lamp and clicked it on.

That's when I saw them.

Eyes. Wide. Bulging. Glaring through a tear in the wallpaper. The floral pattern was peeled back, just slightly, but enough for someone to press their face to the wall. Their eyes locked onto mine, unmoving, unblinking. I stared, paralyzed, before switching the light off again and pulling the blanket over my head like a child. But I wasn't a child. And this wasn't a dream.

A new sound filled the room, dripping.

Soft at first, then louder. A steady *drip... drip... drip...* from somewhere near the wall. I turned the light back on and stepped toward the noise.

Blood.

Thick red drops slid down the wallpaper, soaking into the flowers, staining the wall with horror. I touched it. Sticky. Warm. Real. My fingers trembled.

My mind raced. Alone. Foreign country. Strange hotel. No one to call. No one to trust. I was being watched. Hunted. Played with.

I didn't sleep again. I packed my things in silence as the sky slowly lightened outside. My hands shook. My heart didn't stop pounding. At dawn, I checked out without saying a word and walked until I found another hotel. I still had a week left on my holiday, but I barely left the room after that. I stayed in, locked the doors, and waited for time to pass.

Later, I heard the stories.

About that hotel.

About the man.

They said he wasn't staff. He wasn't even supposed to be there. A former guest. A killer. A predator who had turned the hotel into his hunting ground. He moved through the walls, through the floorboards, watching his victims through holes hidden behind wallpaper. They said he drained them. Murdered them. Left their blood seeping into the very structure of the building.

I had nearly become one of them.

A dream vacation.

A postcard destination.

And a hotel that was nothing more than a tomb waiting to be filled.

House of Hidden Worms in the Walls

We had left the city behind. After decades of noise, neon signs, and concrete blocks, my husband and I finally moved into the peace we'd always dreamed of. A detached house nestled in the countryside, far from crowds or commotion. We were in our sixties, retired, content, and well-off enough to never want for anything. Our days were quiet. Our clothes, elegant. Our car, driven by a chauffeur who arrived on time like clockwork. We were comfortable in every sense of the word. Faithful, too, we went to church every Sunday without fail. The kind of life people worked their whole lives to reach. And we had reached it.

It was autumn when the air first shifted. Not just the seasons, but something else. The sky remained blue, yes, but the wind had a sharpness to it, a warning in its chill. A cold that wasn't just seasonal, it cut. The trees around our home rattled in the breeze, and the sunlight lost its warmth. Winter was coming, and the evenings grew darker by the day. Still, our little home remained our sanctuary.

That night, we were in the lounge, curled together under a shared blanket, watching an old film. Just the two of us, the TV flickering softly in the dark, the house wrapped in silence except for the hum of dialogue from the screen. It was peaceful. Familiar. I felt his hand in mine, and for a moment, I thought, this is the good life.

Then something cold touched my skin.

A slick, slippery trail moved across my arm.

I flinched, brushing it off quickly, telling myself it was my imagination. Maybe a thread, a trick of sensation. I didn't want to think about it too long. I turned my attention back to the movie.

But the feeling returned.

And this time, I saw it.

Out of the corner of my eye, I noticed movement, something small, dark, and wriggling, just at the edge of the wall, where the light of the television flickered faintly.

I sat up slowly.

Shapes.

Slithering shapes, on the walls.

Tiny shadows crawling in silence, like worms stitched into the plaster. I gasped and reached for the lamp, flicking on the light.

And then I screamed.

The walls were alive.

Worms, hundreds of them, thick and pulsing, twisted across the wallpaper like veins under pale skin. The ceiling was moving. The floor was wet. I nearly collapsed, and it was only my husband's arms catching me that kept me from hitting the ground.

They were everywhere.

The walls pulsed with them. The ceiling dripped with them. One landed on my head and slid down my cheek like a ribbon of slime. They began falling faster, writhing in the air as they dropped. My hands flew to my skin, trying to brush them away, but they clung tight, their bodies sticky and warm.

And then, pain.

Sharp. Biting. I looked down and saw them burrowing into my arms, their mouths filled with rows of teeth, gnawing into my flesh. I screamed and thrashed, but they only bit deeper. Blood pooled on my skin as more of them dropped from above, sinking into my neck, my wrists, even my legs. Their eyes, tiny, beady, black, watched without blinking.

My husband tried to help, grabbing them with his hands, flinging them away, but they stuck to him, too. His arms were streaked with blood, his shirt soaked with it. The floor was thick with them now. My ankles were buried, their bodies twisting around each other, slithering up my legs. The sound, oh God, the sound, it was a wet, slapping squelch, constant and close, echoing through the room. I could hear their hunger.

We had to get out.

He pulled me by the arm, dragging me through the swarm toward the door. The worms followed, fast, too fast for something without bones. I looked back once and saw them pouring from the cracks in the ceiling, from the vents, from inside the walls themselves.

The house was infested.

No, possessed.

We made it outside, stumbling into the cold night air. I could still feel them on me. My skin crawled. My legs buckled. But we didn't stop running until we reached the car. That night, we didn't sleep. We called every service we could think of. Exterminators, pest control, even emergency contractors. They came. They saw.

And they left.

Nothing worked. Fumigation failed. Poison didn't kill them. Burning only drove them deeper into the walls. We brought in priests. We burned sage. We prayed. But the worms returned.

And each time, they came back stronger.

More numerous.

Hungrier.

They weren't just feeding on the home. They were feeding on *us*. On blood. On fear. On the flesh of anyone who dared enter.

Eventually, we gave up. We packed what we could and left. We abandoned the house, the walls still squirming behind us. The floor still slick. The air still humming with the sound of their movement.

But sometimes, even now, I hear it.

In my sleep.

In the silence.

Samantha

That wet sound, echoing in memory.

The slither. The gnaw. The endless feeding.

The horror we left behind in that house had roots that went deeper than the foundations. Beneath the floorboards, beneath the walls, there was something unnatural, something wrong. Rotting corpses that had never been buried. A hunger born from the ground itself. The worms didn't just live in the walls.

They *were* the walls.

And they weren't done eating.

Lurking Viper in a Haunted House

It started like a joke. A spur-of-the-moment idea during one of those lazy mornings, when dreams bleed into the day and everything still feels a little surreal. I had woken from a dream so vivid, I could almost still feel it in the air, a haunted house, something old and terrible lurking just out of sight. When I opened my eyes, I laughed softly to myself. And then I sat up and thought: what if?

The idea clung to me all day. A murder mystery weekend, something a little wild and spooky, something to jolt the soul. I looked online, scrolling through places that promised haunted thrills, real-life ghost hunts, stories soaked in legend. Eventually, I found it, a local experience in the woods, advertising an abandoned house known for its bloody past. The photos were eerie, the price was cheap, and it promised a night none of us would forget. I called up a few friends. Excited, skeptical, ready for a thrill. We printed the tickets at home, packed our things, and agreed to meet near the edge of the woods where the whole thing was set to begin.

The day was warm and dry, late spring, with trees beginning to bloom and tiny pink flowers decorating the branches like delicate lace. We gathered under the canopy of fresh leaves, our bags slung over shoulders, our laughter loud and easy. It was meant to be fun. Just fun. We pitched a small tent along the edge of the wooded trail, settled in for the afternoon, and passed the time trading scary stories. One of them chilled the group more than the rest, a tale about an old, bony-faced man who lived in the woods long ago, luring strangers into his crooked house before vanishing them forever. My friend trembled as he retold the story, his voice hushed, his face pale. The fear in his eyes made us laugh at first. We joked, nudged, teased. But the mood shifted.

As the sky turned gold, we gathered ourselves and made the walk toward the house. It stood about twenty minutes beyond the trees, deeper into the woods where the trail turned thin and overgrown. The sun began to dip behind the horizon as we arrived, casting the house in shadow.

Samantha

It was worse than the pictures.

The house sloped unnaturally to the side, its walls bowed, some windows shattered, others boarded. The porch sagged under its own weight, and parts of the roof looked ready to cave. Still, we were buzzing with adrenaline. We stepped forward, eager for a scare.

Then we realized the tickets were fake.

There was no official tour. No host. No welcome. Just the house, waiting.

Still, we couldn't resist. We broke inside.

The floor groaned under our weight. The air smelled damp and old. The stairs creaked like bones underfoot as we wandered deeper. Strange sounds echoed through the empty rooms, whispers, dragging footsteps, thuds from nowhere. As we climbed the stairs, we heard a soft rustling, like breath moving through the walls. My skin prickled.

And then we saw it.

Something white moved through the air across the hallway. Floating. Flickering. No feet. No form. Just a shape in the dark, gliding like mist. We froze, clutching each other, whispering frantic things. The house groaned around us, and suddenly it felt real. Very real.

Then the walls bled.

Dark red liquid oozed from the cracks and corners, running down the wallpaper in thick rivulets. The house shook. Beneath our feet, the floor softened, like it was breathing. Like it was about to give way. We tried to turn back, but our steps were slow, like the ground was pulling us down.

And then it happened.

My friend screamed.

He grabbed his leg, eyes wide, face white. Something had bitten him. We couldn't see it at first, but then a crack of light flashed through a window, like lightning, and we saw it on the floor.

Fear The Bloody Forest In The Dark

A viper.

Large, dark, glistening, its body coiled in the shadows. We froze in horror, our mouths dry, unsure if we were seeing it right. It didn't move like a snake. It pulsed. Twitched. Like it wasn't alive, not in the way animals are. We backed away slowly. My friend's leg was shaking, a welt already rising. We had to get out. We had to get help.

We turned for the door, but it slammed shut in front of us.

Something was in control. Something didn't want us to leave.

The walls rumbled again. The shadows twisted. We screamed, we pushed, we ran, but the house pulled back. The viper was gone. So was the blood. My friend's wound had vanished. It was an illusion. A trick. None of it had been real.

Or maybe it had been, just not in the way we understood.

A voice whispered through the air, low and ancient.

The story of the old man in the woods… it wasn't just a story. He was the one behind it all. He had placed a spell on the land, on the house, on us. The curse was woven into the floorboards and the broken windows. And now it was inside us.

We ran again, out the back, down the hill, into the trees.

But he followed.

We stopped at the edge of the woods, panting, terrified, and there he was, no longer hidden. Red eyes glowing from the tree line. Skin like ash. The air thickened. My friend rose from the ground, lifted by an invisible force, his arms outstretched, his mouth open in silent terror.

The old man, the demon, was casting again.

We couldn't fight it. Not with fists. Not with screaming.

But we remembered the book.

Earlier, in the house, buried beneath a broken floorboard, we had found it, an ancient, mold-eaten book written in a language that didn't belong to any world we knew. We had flipped through it, half-laughing, not realizing what it was. But now we knew. It was the key.

We tore it open again. We chanted the words, screamed them at the sky. Pages tore from our hands. Wind whipped around us. The demon's voice cracked like thunder, angry, shaking the trees. But slowly, slowly, he vanished.

Gone.

The air cleared. The weight lifted.

We dropped the book, left it behind, and we ran. Back to the tent. Back to the safety of noise and fire and ground that didn't try to swallow us.

We never went back.

Not to the woods.

Not to the house.

Not to that cursed trail.

But sometimes, in the silence of night, I still hear his voice. I still see those red eyes. And I know, whatever spell we broke, whatever evil we thought we stopped, it wasn't gone.

Not really.

The Rat in the Sewer

The morning started like any other. Cold. Early. Bleary-eyed and already tired. I'd just finished a night of broken sleep after a long shift, and the alarm hit like a punch to the chest. My body ached. But this was my job, checking the street grids, maintaining the city's underbelly, crawling into the bowels of the sewer system. It wasn't glamorous, and it sure as hell wasn't clean. Just me and the crew, doing the work no one thinks about until the drains back up or the stench hits the air.

I drove the company van in half-awake silence, the heater blasting against the bite of early morning frost. By 7 a.m., I'd parked up and joined the other lads, rough faces, all of us in thick hi-vis coats and boots caked with the dirt of yesterday. We grabbed our gear, checked our headlamps, strapped on our safety hats. The routine always felt the same. Run a check. Test the torches. Share a few words over a thermos of tea and maybe a KitKat if someone remembered to grab one from the garage. Then it was time to go down.

Our job site was at a busy junction in the city centre, one of those old roads built over layers of pipe and concrete, where time had stacked itself one infrastructure at a time. We opened the grid, the steam rolling up with the reek of rot and rust. The smell hit first, thick, meaty, wet. It clung to your nose, your skin, your soul. You never really got used to it. You just learned to breathe through your mouth.

One by one, we descended the ladder into the dark. The cold was worse down there. Colder than the street above, colder than the frost in the air. The tunnels stretched in all directions, narrow, endless veins pumping filth beneath the city. With our headlamps flickering and the distant sound of trickling water echoing all around us, we began the long walk through the tunnels toward the job site.

We were meant to do routine maintenance. Patching, flushing. Nothing special. But something felt off from the start.

The deeper we went, the stranger it got.

Samantha

The tunnel lights, old fluorescent strips bolted high on the ceiling, began to flicker. First one, then another. The darkness crept in like fog. We still had our hat lights, but they didn't last long when you pushed them too hard. And down here, once it went black, it stayed black.

We moved quickly.

And then we heard it.

A sound too faint at first to really place.

A squeak.

A high, sharp squealing, small at first, like a single rat echoing in the distance.

Then another.

And another.

We stopped.

Listened.

The lights overhead went out entirely. Only our headlamps cut through the thick dark now, narrow beams sweeping side to side.

We decided to turn back.

Something was wrong. You didn't ignore your instincts down there. Water could rise without warning. Gasses could collect in air pockets. And now... now something else had started to stir in the dark.

As we retraced our steps, one of the lads let out a shout.

We spun our lights down the corridor and froze.

There it was.

A rat.

But not like any rat I'd ever seen.

It was massive, easily the size of a small dog. Its fur was slick with wet grime, its eyes red, its teeth yellow and long. It was gnawing on something that looked... wrong. And then we saw it. Another rat. A corpse. The big one was eating another rat.

More of them started appearing.

First three. Then seven. Then a swarm, their shapes spilling into the tunnel from side channels and vents. We were surrounded. There was no time to think. We turned and ran, sloshing through water, boots pounding against concrete, trying not to slip.

Then it leapt.

The large rat, the first one, launched itself at one of our crew. He screamed, the sound of it bouncing off the curved walls. The rat landed on his chest, biting into his yellow safety coat. Luckily, the material was thick, thick enough to keep its teeth from reaching flesh. But the fear was real. If it had sunk in, if it had broken the skin... rabies, infection, who knows what else lived in those sewers.

We dragged him off, shouting, running, kicking away the smaller ones that skittered toward our boots. We had no weapons, just a couple of tools. No time to fight. Only time to escape.

The tunnel twisted.

We saw the ladder.

Our exit.

But then came the worst part.

The water.

It began as a trickle, then a rush, then a roar, like a dam had broken somewhere behind us. Dirty, black, fast-moving water flooded the tunnel, rising high around our ankles in seconds.

We hit the ladder, hands slipping on the wet rungs. One by one, we climbed, my boots heavy, my back screaming. The rats kept coming, their squeals louder, closer. The water rose higher. One of the lads was slower, his foot already submerged, the rats circling just below the surface.

And then the grid above wouldn't move.

It was stuck.

Rust. Pressure. Something blocking it.

We screamed to one another. Tools. Use the tools.

A hammer came out. A wrench. We pounded, twisted, yanked with every ounce of desperation in us.

Finally, it gave.

The grid flung open, the smell of fresh air like a punch to the lungs. We spilled out onto the street, panting, soaking, half-mad with adrenaline.

No one was hurt. Somehow. No one bitten. But something had changed in us.

None of us wanted to go back down.

We didn't.

We quit the job. Found safer work. The kind that kept your feet dry and your mind off the dark.

But even now, when I pass over those grids on the pavement, I remember.

The smell. The swarm. The sound of water rushing and the sight of teeth in the dark.

There are things down there no one should ever see.

The city rests above it, moving, buzzing, unaware.

But beneath it, under the streets, in the dark, in the rot and waste, there are tunnels that go deeper than anyone ever mapped.

And something waits down there.

Something still gnawing.

One Way Ticket to Hell

Autumn had settled over the land like a sigh. The air was crisp, the sky dull and grey, and the streets were littered with brittle leaves that crunched beneath every hurried step. Rain had started to fall, cold and relentless, soaking the ground and leaving the leaves soggy underfoot. I had a train to catch.

I rushed through the downpour, weaving between the crowd gathering at the station, all of us strangers driven by purpose. I headed straight for the ticket machine, punched in my destination, and received my ticket. One way. I didn't think much of it at the time. It was meant to be the start of something, an adventure, a break from routine, a holiday after the long slog of autumn work.

When the train arrived, people pushed and jostled to get on board. I found my place by the window, grateful to sink into a seat that promised a decent view for the long journey. The train had a restaurant car, which I found cool, and I had a book to keep me company. It should have been perfect. But the train was packed, people crammed into every aisle and corner. I felt the walls closing in, the heat of too many bodies, and a creeping wave of claustrophobia settled in my chest.

Still, I pressed on, ate something simple, and let the rhythm of the train lull me. I leaned back, pulled my coat tighter, and tried to nap.

That's when I felt it.

A tap on my shoulder, cold and unfamiliar. It startled me awake. I looked around. No one was there.

I brushed it off and lay back again, but before long, another chill touched my skin, like invisible fingers trailing along my back. I sat up, heart hammering. Still, no one. The lights overhead flickered slightly. A sigh escaped me, part exasperation, part unease. I told myself it was just my imagination, but I couldn't ignore the tension coiling in my stomach.

A man walked past my seat, an inspector. His uniform was pressed, his stride deliberate. But something about him was wrong. He didn't look at me, didn't speak. Just passed by like a shadow. My skin prickled as he vanished down the carriage.

Night fell quickly. There were no sleeper berths on this train, which felt odd for such a long journey. Still, my seat was long enough to lie across. I took off my shoes, curled up, and let myself drift again.

Then it came.

I opened my eyes to see a figure standing in the aisle.

Black. Tall. Its face featureless but for two glowing red eyes that locked onto mine with malevolent glee. It didn't move. It didn't speak. It just laughed, low, guttural, and vibrating with malice. My body froze. I couldn't breathe. I was staring at something that didn't belong in this world.

It vanished when I blinked, but the fear remained. I sat bolt upright, wide awake, my heart thundering. I scanned the carriage.

Empty.

Everyone was gone.

The train had been packed. Dozens of passengers, noise, movement, life. But now, I was alone. No footsteps. No murmurs. Just silence and the memory of those eyes.

The realization crashed over me like ice.

This wasn't a normal train.

It was cursed.

Haunted.

Whatever ticket I had bought, it hadn't been for adventure, it had been for damnation. A one-way ride into the unknown, along tracks that led nowhere but down. The darkness outside the window stretched endlessly, a tunnel with no light at the end. Just black. Just death.

I clutched the ticket in my hand. It felt heavier now, like it carried more than paper. It was a passage to somewhere evil.

I didn't sleep again. I didn't blink. I watched every shadow until finally, after what felt like centuries, daylight broke through the window. The train shuddered to a stop.

Relief surged through me, until I stepped off.

The station wasn't right.

It looked normal, but the air was wrong. Heavy. Cold. Voices whispered from the edges, too soft to understand but too clear to be imagined. I ran. I didn't look back. But I knew.

The nightmare wasn't over.

Day and night since that journey, my dreams have been haunted. That figure with red eyes, he visits me still. He waits in corners. Smiles in the dark. A ghost from the hell-bound train that didn't want me to leave.

And sometimes, I wonder if I ever truly did.

Samantha

The Gallows

We lived in the old days, when war echoed through the streets and survival was a daily game of chance. The year was somewhere in the 1940s, and life was hard. Poor wasn't even the word for it, we were on the edge of ruin. Our shoes were falling apart, the soles flapping with every step along the rough cobblestone roads. Our clothes were threadbare, full of holes, stained from the streets, and nothing more than scraps stitched together. I remember feeling like a tramp, wandering the narrow lanes of our crumbling village, the weight of hunger always tugging at my ribs.

The streets were lined with grey stone buildings and soot-covered chimneys. Victorian houses leaned tiredly into one another, their windows fogged from the cold. People bustled past in worn coats and bonnets, their eyes sunken, their expressions always rushing toward something, often the ration line. Vouchers were used instead of coins, war news barked from radios, and disease still lingered like fog in the corners of every room. If you had a cough, you prayed it wasn't the last one.

Crime was high. Everyone was desperate. People stole without shame, food, firewood, anything they could carry. My family was no different. We begged. We took what we could. My relatives were too proud to ask for help, but pride didn't fill your belly. We were ashamed of what we became, but hunger left little room for dignity.

We did have one secret, though. A tunnel, buried beneath our house. It wasn't much, but we made it a shelter. A safe haven. No one else knew about it. It was ours alone, dug by calloused hands and desperation, and in those moments when the air raid sirens howled or the world above felt too cruel, we'd huddle in that cramped space and pretend it was a home.

But one day, everything changed.

Word spread quickly through the village that an execution would take place in the square. Noon. Public. The gallows would be used.

That wasn't so unusual back then. Death was always near, and the rope was still a punishment the law didn't shy away from. Executions weren't private affairs. They were meant to be seen, to remind people that justice, no matter how brutal, would always find you.

We gathered, like everyone else, in the heart of the village. The air was thick with smoke and cold mist. Children stood on their parents' shoulders. Old men lit pipes with shaking hands. Some watched in silence. Others looked away.

The prisoner was brought out from the local jail.

A young woman.

She wore black, dress, bonnet, shoes. Her hands were bound. She didn't cry. She didn't beg. She walked with a strange calm, the kind that made your stomach twist.

They led her up the steps. Her head was covered. The noose placed tight around her neck. The auctioneer, a grim man with shaking hands, prepared the lever.

I watched. Everyone did.

When he pulled the handle, the trapdoor opened and the girl dropped.

But it didn't go smoothly.

Her body jolted and twisted violently, blood pouring from her nose, mouth, her skin rupturing, painting the wooden platform beneath her in long streaks of crimson. The crowd gasped as her body convulsed, her legs kicking in a grotesque dance of death. It wasn't quick. It wasn't clean.

Then a man stepped forward and, without a word, raised a blade and severed her head.

Blood sprayed in a red arc across the stone. Her body was left dangling, headless, a torn mess of bone and flesh. The horror was complete.

People screamed. Some ran. Others stood frozen. I couldn't look away. Her spine, white and clean, was visible through the shredded muscle of her neck. Her bones looked like sculpture. But this wasn't art. It was punishment.

They left her hanging for days.

The flesh peeled slowly from her face in the cold autumn air. Birds came and pecked. Flies circled like black halos. Her body turned to something else, something not human anymore. A message.

Her crime?

Arsenic.

She poisoned five people, her own family. Not quickly. Not mercifully. She dismembered them one by one. Used the parts to make stew. Sold it to local shops.

People had eaten it.

She never wanted their money. Only death. Only their suffering.

And she got her punishment, swinging from a rope on the gallows, then chopped to pieces, then left to rot in front of all of us.

They burned her bones eventually. Scattered the ashes. But even ash doesn't kill evil.

To this day, they say her spirit walks the cobblestone streets, drifting past the narrow lanes at night. A black figure with no face, a red mist clinging to her like a veil. People cross themselves when they pass the square. They say she brings sickness. Misfortune. Screams in the dark.

And strangely... our family was never poor after that.

One of her remaining relatives, wealthy beyond belief, took pity on us. Or maybe guilt. They helped lift us out of the gutter. Maybe it was blood money. Maybe it was penance. Either way, our tunnel became a proper home. Our shoes were new. Our clothes, warm.

But it never felt like a blessing.

Not when evil had paid the price.

We still had witches among us. Still had cursed blood. Even now, people fear walking alone on those narrow streets. The war might have ended, but fear never left.

Not in that village.

Not after her.

A Snake on a Cross on an Abandoned Farm

Spring had bloomed with its usual charm. The days were warmer, and the sunlight stretched lazily across the open countryside. The air smelled of fresh grass, damp soil, and something clean, something hopeful. We had packed up and headed out to the farm for what we thought would be another peaceful family holiday. The kind of holiday where life slowed down, where muddy boots and hay-filled barns replaced screens and city noise. My children were excited beyond measure.

We were staying in the old farmhouse, a two-storey building with warped wooden steps and creaky floors that felt more charming than inconvenient. The windows framed long stretches of green farmland, and the scent of livestock and turned earth drifted in through the open shutters. My kids took to it immediately, throwing themselves into the farm life without a second thought. They loved petting the animals, especially the lambs and sheep. There was one goat in particular they became obsessed with, a white one named Billy.

Billy was a character. Always in trouble, always escaping the pen, always chewing on someone's sleeve or trying to climb into the back of the tractor. The kids adored him. He made them laugh until their stomachs hurt. Their wellies were constantly covered in mud, their faces smeared with straw, and their clothes full of hay. They'd roll around in the barn, giggling until they couldn't breathe. For them, this was paradise.

Every year, we chose the farm over any other destination. No beaches. No theme parks. Just the countryside and its quiet simplicity. And each time we returned, it felt like slipping into an old, familiar storybook.

But this year, the story changed.

One morning, the sun was already hot by the time we stepped out into the fields. There was barely a breeze, just the soft rustle of crops swaying in the distance. We had joined the farmhands to help pick sprouts from the warm soil. It was peaceful, almost too quiet. As we moved further into the fields, we came to a part of the property that the owners said had once been abandoned, then recently reclaimed. It looked like any other patch of land, until we saw it.

A wooden cross.

It stood tall and weathered in the middle of the field, as if it had grown out of the earth overnight. No markings. No explanation. Just raw, cracked timber, leaning slightly to one side. The farm owners were just as confused as we were, they claimed they'd never seen it before. They swore it wasn't there yesterday.

Something about it made my skin crawl. The way it stood alone, the way it didn't belong. It didn't feel like a grave or a marker. It felt like a warning.

We moved closer, cautiously, curiosity winning out over instinct.

Then we saw it.

Wrapped around the base of the cross was something long, black, and alive. It was sleek and quick, its forked tongue darting through the air with menace. It hissed as it slithered along the wood, and then we saw the eyes, sharp, soulless, and locked on us.

A snake.

Not just any snake, a black mamba.

I'd read about them. Usually grey in colour. One of the deadliest snakes in the world. It wasn't native to this country. It shouldn't have been anywhere near a British farm. But it was real. Real, and fast.

It moved in a flash, lunging forward before any of us could scream.

And it bit my youngest child.

The scream that tore out of my throat didn't even sound human. I scooped him into my arms as panic took over. The farm, the fields, the sunshine, everything blurred. My child was going limp, his skin pale, sweat breaking across his brow. My heart raced so fast I thought it would burst. We ran.

Samantha

Back to the farmhouse, screaming for help, begging for someone, anyone, to come. But there was no one. The house was empty. No staff. No guests. Just silence and shadows. We pounded on doors. We yelled into rooms. Nothing.

It was as if the people we'd been talking to all week had never existed.

We had no phone. No reception. No help.

I held my boy close, watching the life flicker in his eyes, and I knew we were running out of time. We left the house and ran into the road, calling out, waving our arms like mad people.

And then, as if from nowhere, a van pulled up.

A man stepped out, calm, silent, focused. He didn't ask questions. Just opened the door and drove like he'd been waiting for us. The road twisted and curved, trees flying past, time folding in on itself. We arrived at the hospital just in time.

They took my boy in immediately. He was barely conscious, his breathing shallow. They injected the anti-venom. Hooked him up to machines. I sat in the corner, praying.

Hours passed. Then they told us he would live.

The relief hit me like a wave. I wept and held his hand, whispering over and over how brave he'd been, how strong. But the questions lingered.

What was a black mamba doing on a farm in the UK?

How did it get there?

Why was it wrapped around a cross that had never been there before?

We went back to the farmhouse a few days later, only to find it boarded up.

The place was abandoned again.

The cross was gone.

The people we thought we'd seen, the ones we'd talked to, laughed with, shared meals with, they had vanished. No records. No trace. Just the animals, quietly grazing as if nothing had ever happened.

Somewhere deep inside, I knew the truth.

That wasn't a normal farm.

It was something else.

A ghostly place with the face of a holiday, but the heart of something darker. That cross had summoned more than just curiosity, it had summoned death. And if it weren't for that man in the van, we might not have escaped it.

We never went back to any farm after that. Not even for a visit.

And to this day, I still wonder who saved us.

And who, or what, had set the snake on the cross.

The Bible

The sun streamed through the hotel window, casting golden light across the tiled floor. I stirred slowly, the warmth of the Jerusalem morning washing over me. It was my first day of holiday in the holy city, and already I could hear the buzz of life outside, voices rising in Arabic, footsteps echoing in narrow streets, and the faint call to prayer drifting on the breeze.

I sat up in bed, took a moment to breathe it all in, and smiled. There was something sacred about this place, the whitewashed buildings, the ancient mosques, the echo of devotion that seemed to hum through every stone. The smell of food from nearby stalls floated through the open window, spices, grilled meats, fresh bread. My stomach growled in response.

I decided not to eat at the hotel. I wanted to explore, to walk through the city, to see and feel everything for myself. I took a quick shower, dressed in my loose prayer clothes and sandals, and headed out into the sun-soaked streets. The light was sharp and clean. Donkeys trotted past, pulling carts. The shopkeepers were already shouting their prices. I wandered without direction, drinking in the noise, the colours, the ancient life of the city.

That's when I saw it.

A small, tucked-away shop barely visible between two larger buildings. Its windows were dusty, its sign worn with age. Inside, it looked more like a relic than a store, wooden shelves stacked with faded books and strange artifacts. Something drew me in.

The air inside was thick with age, the scent of paper and incense lingering. As I browsed, my eyes landed on an old bible resting on a crooked stand near the back. The cover was rusted with time, and on the front was an image of Jesus nailed to the cross. Something about it pulled at me. I picked it up, it was heavy, the leather cracked beneath my fingers. Without thinking twice, I carried it to the counter.

The man behind the desk looked at me with strangely calm eyes. As he wrapped the book in brown paper, he said, "Enjoy your book. It has special powers."

I gave him a half-smile. "What do you mean by that?"

He said nothing more.

I tucked the bible under my arm and left, more amused than alarmed. Maybe it was just part of the sales pitch. Still, I felt something off about the way he'd said it.

I found a little café nearby and sat outside under an umbrella. The city moved around me, pilgrims, tourists, shopkeepers, and worshippers weaving together in a beautiful, chaotic rhythm. I ordered a spiced coffee and a chapti wrap with eggs. As I ate, I glanced at the bible still wrapped on the table, but didn't open it. I was too content to disrupt the peace.

After breakfast, I wandered again, eventually arriving at one of the city's historic mosques. It was nearly 11 a.m. when I joined the worshippers. The room was full, kneeling, bowing, praying in quiet unison. I stayed for thirty minutes, letting the stillness of the space settle into my bones.

When I stepped back outside, the city was baking under the midday sun. I walked a little further until I reached the site believed to be where Jesus had once hung on the cross. Tourists swarmed the space, snapping photos. I didn't have a camera. I sat near the spot and just observed, thinking, breathing, feeling. There was something heavy about the place, like a weight pressing against your chest. I stayed for thirty minutes, then made my way back to the hotel.

Once in my room, I collapsed onto the bed with a cold bottle of water and finally unwrapped the book.

The bible felt colder than it should have in the warm room. Its pages were yellowed, delicate, but readable. I flicked through slowly, absorbing the strange energy radiating off the paper. Then I noticed something.

Samantha

Red ink.

It bled across the page in jagged writing:

"Jesus on a cross.

The blood will rush as I'm hung to die.

My spirit will live in pain.

A devil will haunt the one who left me to die."

I stared at the words, unsure if I was reading scripture or something else entirely. My skin prickled.

I kept turning pages.

The red ink returned, this time darker. Thicker.

"Whoever reads this book…

A death will occur.

The devil will rise for the death of Jesus."

A chill ran down my spine.

I snapped the book shut.

But I couldn't stay away from it.

That night, after the city had quieted and the prayers had echoed into silence, I found myself drawn back to the bible. I had gone out for a night walk, passing the same streets, the same mosques, eating an ice cream across from the prayer halls. I had felt peaceful again, until I returned to the hotel.

I sat on the edge of the bed, turned on the bedside lamp, and opened the book again.

This time, the message screamed from the page.

"This page is dangerous.

The nails are ready.

The cross is prepared.

Fear The Bloody Forest In The Dark

Blood will drain.

Food will rot.

Don't fall asleep.

The devil will rise.

Your death will come."

I froze.

The air in the room thickened, heat pressing against my chest like a weight. Panic settled in.

I had to destroy it.

I grabbed the book and began tearing pages. They ripped like fabric, each one screaming louder in my hands. A voice, deep and demonic, erupted from between the pages. It wasn't imagined. It was real. It yelled, laughed, spat curses at me.

Blood began to seep from the pages.

Actual blood.

I kept tearing, throwing sheets across the room, heart pounding in my throat. The laughter turned to screams. The room grew darker, colder.

And then, silence.

The book was in pieces.

The blood stopped.

But something still lingered in the room. A shadow that didn't belong. A whisper that hadn't died.

Jesus wasn't the only presence in that book. Something else had lived in those words, something ancient, something twisted. A devil hidden in scripture. A trap laid in holy disguise.

I had escaped. Just barely.

But sometimes, late at night, I still hear the laughter.

Snorkeling In the Deep Ocean

Today was finally the day. The day I'd been dreaming about for weeks, my holiday to the vast, magical ocean. I was buzzing with excitement but also feeling a flicker of nervousness deep inside. The ocean was beautiful, yes, but also mysterious and unknown. I was about to go snorkeling just off a small island in St. Lucia, in the Caribbean. The thought of diving beneath the waves, swimming alongside sea life, sent my mind spinning with wonder.

I spent most of the morning packing, double-checking every little thing. My flight was in the evening, which suited me perfectly. I preferred flying at night, the sky quieter, the world softer when the sun wasn't glaring down. I could almost feel the peaceful hum of the plane above the clouds already, and my heart was light, like I was floating on air.

By afternoon, I settled into the calm of home, catching up on local news on TV. I wasn't traveling alone. Macy, my girlfriend, was with me, and together we shared the excitement, the small moments before a big adventure.

At 4 p.m., it was time to leave. The drive to the airport was a mix of laughter and quiet anticipation. We checked in our suitcases, careful not to forget anything important. The airport buzzed with its usual energy, but stepping into the air-conditioned departure lounge was like entering a cool oasis. The soft hum of the air and the gentle clinking of cups from the nearby café made waiting almost pleasant.

We had about an hour before boarding, so we wandered through the duty-free shops. Macy picked up some facial cream and a small bottle of Anaïs Anaïs perfume, French, delicate, something that smelled like the ocean breeze I was chasing. I grabbed some snacks, drinks, and a bottle of aftershave. The little rituals of travel, small comforts before the unknown.

Finally, the announcement came. Our flight number was called, and we queued at gate 14. The plane was a large Boeing 767, humming quietly as the ground crew loaded the last of the luggage. Boarding passes checked, passports scanned, we stepped onto the aircraft with a thrill.

Our seats were near the front, just by the toilets, a small comfort if you ask me. As everyone settled, the captain's voice came over the speakers, warm and steady, announcing our imminent takeoff. The safety demonstration followed, the cabin crew moving with practiced ease. Then the engines roared to life, and we pushed back from the gate. The wheels began to roll, faster and faster, until with a gentle lurch, we lifted into the night sky.

My ears popped, and I couldn't help but laugh softly. We were on our way to St. Lucia.

The first few hours were calm. Drinks were served, I chose water, keeping clear-headed. The meal came, but an unexpected commotion broke the calm: a fight between two female passengers. The crew moved swiftly, and the troublemakers were escorted off before we landed.

Touching down in St. Lucia, the airport felt cool against the warm night outside. We grabbed our bags and stepped into the tropical breeze, hot, but softened by a gentle wind. A taxi was waiting to take us to the local dock, where the real adventure would begin.

The taxi ride was a blur of warm air and soft island sounds, ferrying us to the local dock. The scent of salt and sea wrapped around us, promising the adventure ahead. We stepped onto the wooden pier, the night sky mirrored in the gentle waves lapping beneath us. Renting snorkeling gear wasn't cheap, but nothing could dampen my excitement.

We boarded a boat to the island where our hotel awaited, dropped off our luggage, and then set off again, this time heading for another nearby island, the true gateway to the ocean's secrets.

Changing into wetsuits was an odd mix of chilly and snug. The crew guided us patiently, demonstrating how to use the breathing masks and teaching us the basics of diving safely. It was reassuring to know we wouldn't be alone once we plunged beneath the waves.

Then, finally, we dived in.

The ocean welcomed us like an ancient, liquid world. As we sank deeper, the sunlight dimmed, and the blue grew darker, richer, alive. Whales sang their haunting songs nearby. Schools of fish, brilliant and shimmering, darted between coral like living jewels. And there, a serpent of the sea, winding gracefully through the water, a creature of myth come to life.

But wonder was quickly shadowed by fear.

A great white shark glided into view, massive and commanding. My heart hammered hard against my ribs, a surge of adrenaline flooding my veins. The ocean had turned from a dreamscape to a test of courage. Still, we pressed on, swimming deeper, the thrill and terror entwined.

Ahead, the mouth of a cave yawned wide and dark. We entered with our flashlights cutting through the blackness. A crackling radio buzzed faintly at our sides, our lifeline in this underwater wilderness.

Inside, serpents swarmed, weaving between jagged rocks like shadows come alive. And worse, a huge shark, blocking our only way out.

Panic rose fast, clawing at my mind. The cramped space magnified every breath, every heartbeat. I felt my muscles tense, chest tightening, the slow creep of claustrophobia squeezing my thoughts. I forced myself to stay calm, steady my breathing. The shark's eyes burned with anger, refusing to move.

We fired a flare, its flickering light casting wild shadows, but it didn't budge. Desperation drove me to call out on the emergency radio, crackling and broken, a faint hope someone would hear us.

Time slipped away, air thinning around us.

Then, a glimmer, a narrow gap in the cave's wall. We swam swiftly, weaving past the writhing serpents. The gap was tight, but freedom was closer than fear. We squeezed through just as the cave collapsed behind us with a thunderous roar, sealing the shark inside.

The rush of open water welcomed us back, the surface a shining promise after the nightmare below.

We broke through the surface, gasping for air, hearts pounding with relief and lingering fear. Our boat waited nearby, faces tense with worry as we climbed aboard. We explained what had happened, the cave, the serpents, the shark, our words tumbling out in a rush, desperate to make sense of the terror we'd just escaped.

Despite the nightmare, we decided to swim again. Maybe to prove to ourselves that the ocean wasn't all danger, that there was still beauty beneath the waves.

But the ocean had other plans.

A great white shark burst through the ripples, eyes blazing with fury, slicing through the water like a shadow of death. We swam for our lives, muscles burning, hearts slamming against ribs, every stroke driven by raw, primal fear.

As if the shark wasn't enough, a storm rolled in suddenly, thunder cracking like the sky was breaking open, lightning fracturing the dark clouds. The island was surrounded by raging seas and predators beneath the surface.

We fled back to the safety of the hotel, soaked and shaken. The warmth of the room was a fragile shield against the chaos outside. And yet, the fear lingered, heavy and raw.

It was only our second day on the island, but we knew the rest of the trip had been stolen from us.

With trembling hands, we rebooked our flight home.

Because some experiences leave marks deeper than any holiday memory.

Because no one should have to face the hell of being trapped, alone and helpless, beneath the cold, dark ocean.

Secret Cove on The Beach

It was one of those sweltering summer nights where the air outside is dry, but inside, it clings to your skin like a thick, invisible blanket. The room was still and sticky, not a whisper of breeze to offer relief. I tossed and turned, struggling to find sleep, but a strange feeling began to build inside me, a good vibe, like a gentle nudge telling me to go somewhere, to escape.

In my restless mind, I drifted into a dream of a hidden cove on a deserted beach. Smooth, rounded budge rocks dotted the shore, with tiny pools of shimmering water catching the sunlight. The place felt magical, a secret world waiting just beyond reach. The heat was relentless, so I kept my window open and the fan blowing, but the dream pulled me deeper, insisting I keep going.

Morning came fast. I dashed out of bed, rushing to the shower, letting the cool water wash away the night's sweat. My body was sticky and warm from the heat, but the shower brought a refreshing clarity. After breakfast, I made the bed and decided to scroll through holiday websites, drawn to the idea of that mysterious cove from my dream.

There it was, a deserted beach, just like I imagined. I didn't hesitate. I called my friend Lucy. She answered immediately, her excitement matching mine. Lucy was the beach lover between us, always chasing the sun and waves, and a bit of a poser with her modelling career. We quickly booked a week-long getaway at the beach with secret coves, thanks to a cancellation that made it possible.

Packing was a rush of energy. I grabbed my things upstairs while Lucy did the same. She came over to stay at my place, and we had a small celebration, pizza, a few drinks, and a horror movie marathon featuring *The Evil Dead*, her favorite. We weren't romantically involved, just close friends sharing an adventure.

Before long, the day of departure arrived. We flew out on an afternoon flight, navigating check-in and security with practiced ease. The departure lounge was a cool refuge, and we browsed the duty-free shops where Lucy scored a bottle of Dior Poison, always hunting for a bargain.

Our flight was busy, the plane filled with passengers, but soon we were strapped in, engines humming as we taxied down the runway. The sun shone brightly as we lifted off, leaving the world behind and heading toward sun, sea, and the hidden coves of Portugal.

By the third day, the excitement of exploration had taken hold. Lucy and I had checked into our hotel and spent the first couple of days soaking up sun and sea, but now it was time to find the secret cove from my dream.

After some searching, we found it, a secluded spot where the water gleamed a deep, inviting blue, framed by jagged budge rocks and just a small sandy patch. The cove was shadowed, the sunlight barely reaching the water's surface, giving it a mysterious, almost otherworldly feel.

Without hesitation, we slipped into the water, feeling its cool embrace against our sun-warmed skin. We decided to swim naked, Lucy was shy at first, but she talked me into it, part of the freedom the cove offered.

Then, suddenly, everything changed.

Underneath the water, sharp pain exploded in Lucy's leg. She cried out, blood rushing into the clear water like ink. I glanced down in horror and saw two distinct fang marks sinking deep into her skin.

Panic flared. The cove was filling fast with a strong current, pulling us toward the narrow sandy patch. We scrambled through the dark water, urgency sharpening every movement.

Lucy's leg throbbed violently, the venom from the sea snake biting deep. She wiped at the blood streaming down, her heart pounding as fear clawed at her mind.

There was no way to call for help, we were stuck on an island with no signal.

But then, hope.

Samantha

A boat's distant engine whispered across the water.

Lucy panicked, but I urged calm. Panicking would only spread the venom faster. I helped her steady herself as we fought the current together, swimming desperately toward the shore.

We reached the sand just as the boat ran aground. I shouted for help, and a man appeared, rushing to carry Lucy onto the boat.

With relief, we set off toward the local town, the boat slicing through the waves as Lucy lay pale but alive beside me.

The ride to the local town felt endless, every wave rocking us closer to safety. At the hospital, Lucy was rushed inside, the hours stretching into days as doctors worked to heal the venom's damage. When she finally emerged, pale but alive, relief washed over me like a tide.

We returned to our hotel with only one day left to savor. The trauma still lingered, but we forced ourselves to enjoy the local village, shopping for little treasures, laughing over bargains, and indulging in a meal at a cozy fish restaurant, Lucy's favorite.

The next morning came too quickly. We packed our things, checked out, and took a taxi back to the airport. Security and duty-free shopping felt familiar but distant as our minds clung to the events that had shaken us.

Boarding the plane, we felt the weight of the holiday's shadow despite the sunny skies outside.

Back home, the cove remained etched in my memory, magical yet hiding a lurking horror beneath its surface. There were no signs warning visitors about the hidden danger beneath the water. What should have been a dream holiday turned into a nightmare we would never forget. Lucy's leg had healed, but the fear stayed with her, a quiet reminder that some places hold secrets not meant to be disturbed.

Since then, we've left beach holidays behind, trading sand and sea for the safety of city breaks, where the only bites we risk are from the cold breeze, not a slithering creature beneath the waves.

Black Lake Forest

The day had been unusually quiet, with nothing much stirring beyond the slow passing of hours. My mind wandered, craving an adventure, not one that took us far away or into chaos, but something close, simple, and wild. Roxanne, my girlfriend, was always the perfect partner for this kind of escape. She thrived outdoors, fearless and ready to push limits. So we talked, tossing around ideas, until the plan was clear: a weekend camping trip to somewhere local, somewhere quiet.

The thought of no deadlines, no work calls, no distractions was pure freedom. We packed our camping gear with enthusiasm, tent, sleeping bags, a modest stash of food and supplies. Roxanne's excitement was infectious; she practically bounced as we loaded the car. No kids, no commitments, just two people and the promise of the wild.

Friday evening rolled in faster than I expected. We kept it low-key, knowing an early start awaited us. Sleep came quickly, although my mind was buzzing with anticipation, filled with images of towering trees and crackling campfires.

Before dawn broke, we were awake. The sky outside was still a soft pink, the first light bleeding gently across the horizon. The air felt crisp and fresh, untouched by the day's heat. We washed quickly, shared a simple breakfast, and packed the last few items into the car. The lock clicked shut behind us, a small but significant gesture marking the start of our escape.

The drive to Black Lake Forest took about an hour, the scenery shifting as we left suburban calm for the embrace of nature. Soon, the dense forest came into view: rows upon rows of towering pine trees, their dark trunks rising like silent sentinels against the sky.

We parked on a narrow dirt road edged by thick undergrowth. The forest air was heavy and scented with pine and earth. We carefully unloaded our camping gear, securing the car and locking it tight. Every sound, the rustle of leaves, the crunch of pine needles beneath our feet, felt magnified in the stillness.

The winding path into the woods was long and dusty, twisting deeper between the tall pines that crowded so close it felt like they were swallowing the sky. Light filtered weakly through the thick canopy, casting long shadows and giving everything a muted, almost eerie glow.

After a steady walk, we found a small clearing, just enough space to set up camp. The ground was soft underfoot, blanketed in needles and moss. We pitched the tent carefully, the fabric stretching tight and secure. The quiet was almost deafening, broken only by the distant call of a bird or the whisper of wind through the branches.

We settled inside the tent for a brief rest, savoring the peacefulness of being alone in the heart of the forest. But the pull of the wild was strong. Soon, we grabbed our flashlights and decided to explore further, venturing deeper into the shadows where the forest thickened, and the mysteries grew.

As we pushed further into the forest, the thick canopy swallowed what little light the fading afternoon had offered. The path grew narrower, twisting and turning like a tangled serpent. Every step kicked up dust and dry pine needles, the sound muffled by the dense air. Our flashlights barely pierced the growing shadows, casting long, jittery beams that flickered against the towering trunks.

The forest's stillness was almost unnatural. No birdsong, no rustling of small animals, just the steady crunch of our footsteps and the occasional whisper of wind teasing through the pine needles. It felt like the trees themselves were watching, their shadows deepening into shapes that seemed to shift just beyond the edge of vision.

A cold shiver traced down my spine, the hairs on my neck rising as I sensed something watching us. Then, out of the corner of my eye, I caught a glimpse, a tall, twisted shadow standing motionless between the trees. It was far too large to be human, with limbs that stretched at impossible angles and a presence that screamed danger.

Fear The Bloody Forest In The Dark

Its eyes, if you could call them that, glowed with a chilling, otherworldly light, fixed upon us with a cold, malevolent hunger. My heart slammed against my ribs as fear gripped me, raw and immediate.

I glanced at Roxanne; her wide eyes mirrored my terror. We were utterly unarmed, vulnerable in this vast wilderness. The stories she had once whispered about the forest, creatures that only came at night, lurking deep in the pine's shadows, now felt horrifyingly real.

We knew the creature could hear every sound, smell every breath. Any noise might draw it closer. Our voices caught in our throats; we dared not shout or scream.

Suddenly, the creature lunged.

We ran blindly, feet pounding the hard earth as branches whipped against our faces. Desperation lent speed to our flight as we scrambled toward the nearest trees. Without hesitation, we climbed, fingers digging into rough bark, branches scraping our skin but offering the only refuge.

Above us, the creature's growls filled the night air, guttural and furious. It clawed at the trunk, claws digging deep, splintering bark beneath its grip. Blood dripped from its snarling jaws, glistening in the faint moonlight.

Just as relief flickered in our hearts, more shapes emerged from the darkness, other creatures, their teeth razor-sharp, eyes wild with hunger. They circled below like a pack of wolves, but their forms were twisted and unnatural. Fear rooted us to the branches, breath shallow and rapid.

We huddled close, every muscle trembling as the night stretched on, each minute an eternity under the cold gaze of the forest's monstrous inhabitants.

The night dragged on, a relentless blur of growls and scratching that echoed in the stillness. The creatures circled relentlessly, their hunger palpable, their eyes glowing like embers in the dark. We were trapped, perched high in the tree, frozen in place, with nowhere to run or hide.

Samantha

Every minute felt like an hour as the pack prowled beneath us. The forest seemed to close in tighter, suffocating, whispering of dangers beyond imagining. Roxanne clung to me, trembling, her breath ragged. I felt the weight of helplessness crushing down on us, knowing that we were at the mercy of these unearthly predators.

Just as the first blush of dawn began to seep through the branches, salvation arrived in the form of a group of men. They moved silently but swiftly, armed with guns that gleamed under the dim light. The sharp cracks of gunfire shattered the eerie silence, each shot cutting through the night and striking down the creatures one by one.

The nightmare that had held us captive was finally broken.

The men reached us quickly, their faces calm but serious as they guided us down from the tree. Every step felt surreal, the forest still heavy with the echoes of what had passed. We hurried back to our campsite, packing our belongings with trembling hands, hearts still pounding from the terror.

Their presence was a shield, a lifeline back to safety. They helped us to the car, the forest's dark menace retreating with each mile we put behind us.

That night in Black Lake Forest was a living nightmare, a battle for survival against creatures that defied explanation. We had been lucky, blessed to see the men who came to our rescue just in time.

Though the forest still holds its secrets deep in the shadows, we carry the scars of that night, memories of fear and helplessness etched into our bones. We survived the claws and teeth of the unknown, but the experience changed us forever.

The Letter Box Killer

The alarm buzzed sharply at 4 a.m., pulling me from a restless sleep into the biting cold of a winter morning. The sky outside was an icy gray, thick with frost that glazed everything in a hard, unforgiving glaze. Even before stepping outside, I could feel the chill creeping through the thin walls of my house, settling deep into my bones.

I was a postal worker, my job started early, and today was no different. By 6 a.m., I needed to be at the depot, ready to face the long, tiring hours ahead. Sorting through mountains of mail for the local neighborhood was exhausting enough, but my duties didn't stop there. I'd spend countless hours walking up and down stairs, delivering letters to every doorstep, and some days, I had to drive the van to deliver parcels scattered across the estates.

The physical toll was heavy. My legs ached by midday, my back stiff from hauling bags of mail, but this was the job, a routine I knew well, even if some days brought unease.

Emptying post boxes was part of the risk. You never knew what might be hidden inside, it could be nothing but letters and bills, or it could be something dangerous. That uncertainty was a constant shadow, lurking behind every metal box.

Today, I was assigned to the van, responsible for loading parcels and emptying those same post boxes, but this time from the safety of my vehicle. The early morning air was miserable, damp and cold enough to fog my breath, and I kept the heater cranked high inside the van, the engine's hum a small comfort against the chill.

As I drove through the local estates, the roads slick with ice, I kept my eyes sharp, my mind on the task ahead. The day stretched long and slow before me, hours of routine stops, mail to collect and deliver, and the ever-present weight of the unknown hidden inside those postal boxes.

By 9:30 a.m., I was deep into my rounds, the van rattling along icy roads as the cold bit through the windows. The heater was cranked high, but it barely kept the chill at bay. The winter morning was miserable, gray skies pressing down, the kind of day that seemed to drain the color from everything.

The routine was mechanical by now. Stop. Open the post box. Empty the mail. Repeat. But today, something felt off. A strange prickling ran down my spine, a warning I couldn't shake. When I pulled up to a familiar cluster of boxes, my hand hesitated over the lock. I told myself it was nothing, just nerves, and pulled open the door.

What I saw inside made my blood run cold.

Something wriggled, coiled tight in the shadows of the metal box. I could hear a rattling sound, sharp and alarming. My heart slammed against my ribs as sweat broke out on my forehead despite the cold. My fingers fumbled, trying to grab the mail, but the creature moved, the unmistakable hiss rising from deep inside its coils.

Suddenly, it lashed out, a flash of motion, a sharp nip on my face. I jumped back, staggering, my skin burning where it bit. The venom was real, and the danger immediate.

Panic took hold. I slammed the post box shut, my breath ragged. I called emergency services, my voice trembling as I notified my boss. The world around me spun into chaos, blue lights flashing as the ambulance rushed me to the hospital, sirens screaming into the cold air.

My face began to swell, the pain unbearable, a fiery, throbbing torment that felt like torture. Doctors and nurses swarmed, hooking me up to IV lines, pumping in antivenom as fast as they could. I was helpless, trapped in a nightmare where every second counted.

I knew then that I wouldn't be back to work anytime soon, this injury would keep me sidelined for at least a week, maybe longer.

Lying helpless in the hospital bed, the weight of what had happened settled heavily on me. The venom had left its mark, not just the swelling and scars that mottled my face, but the fear that gnawed relentlessly at my mind. Every heartbeat echoed the memory of pain and panic, and every shadow seemed to carry the threat of danger.

While the doctors worked tirelessly to heal my body, I wrestled with a growing sense of unease. The job I once knew, walking the quiet streets, emptying mailboxes, now felt like a trap. The very act of handling letters, something so mundane before, had become a source of anxiety. My hands trembled, sweat poured down my brow, and a creeping phobia took hold whenever I thought of delivering mail again.

The nightmares came with the night, restless and vivid. Sleep became elusive, replaced by sleepless hours haunted by rattling boxes and sharp, fanged creatures lurking in the shadows. I told myself over and over: I'm alive. I'm alive. But the scars ran deeper than skin.

It was during those long, painful days that I made a decision. I handed in my notice. The fear, the trauma, they were too much. I needed a fresh start.

Soon after, I found a new path, managing a local restaurant. The warm smells of cooking food, the lively chatter of customers, the buzz of a busy kitchen, it was a world apart from the cold, dangerous mail routes. Here, I found a sense of peace I hadn't known in months.

Though the scars on my face remained, and the memories lingered, I was determined to reclaim my life. The nightmares might return, and the fear might never fully disappear, but I was alive. And sometimes, that was enough.

The Tunnel

It was a Saturday evening in early spring, the kind of night that hinted at new beginnings. I was about to head off on a holiday with some friends, and even though our flight wasn't until the early hours of Sunday morning, there was this buzzing excitement in the air that made it feel like the adventure had already started.

We made sure to double-check our tickets and passports, no way was I forgetting those, and kept reminding ourselves how lucky we were. The destination was the Caribbean, but that was about all I knew. Jimmy, one of the guys in the group, had been tight-lipped about the exact location. It was a surprise planned for my 40th birthday, a gift from all my friends who chipped in together. The thought alone made me smile, such a cool gesture.

Around 7 PM, we decided to stop at the local convenience store to grab snacks for the plane. Airport prices were ridiculous, and no one wanted to pay triple for a bag of chips or a bottle of water. We picked up a few things, chatting about what awaited us, the warm sun, blue skies, and the endless sea. I kept imagining the quiet island we'd be staying on, with hardly anyone else around. I wasn't sure where exactly we'd be landing, but I knew the hotel was booked and waiting for us somewhere beautiful.

After the quick stop, we got back into the car and started driving toward the airport. The road was quiet and familiar, but then Jimmy suddenly realized he'd taken a wrong turn. We joked about it at first, "No big deal, we'll just go back", but as we turned around, it became clear we'd ended up at a dead end. Right there, just ahead of us, was a dark tunnel, with a warning sign standing tall beside it.

Curiosity got the better of us, so we all stepped out of the car. Since the sun was still up, no one thought to grab a torch or any extra light. Jimmy, Kai, and I decided to walk down into the tunnel. It felt strange, like stepping into another world. The air inside was cooler, and the faint sounds of the evening echoed around us.

That's where it all started, a wrong turn, a mysterious tunnel, and the beginning of an experience none of us would ever forget.

As we made our way deeper into the tunnel, the sounds above grew louder, like a train rushing by on the tracks overhead. It was an odd feeling, standing beneath all that noise, with shadows dancing on the rough walls around us.

Suddenly, without warning, there was a huge bang, followed by a loud crash. We turned just in time to see the entrance behind us collapse. A pile of rubble blocked the way out. We were trapped.

Panic hit us immediately. No phones, no way to call for help. No water or snacks either. Just the dark, the cold tunnel, and the growing sense that we had messed up badly.

We sat there in silence at first, the reality sinking in that we would definitely miss our flight, and worse, our holiday. Hours dragged on. The night stretched before us like a nightmare. The excitement we'd felt just hours earlier was replaced by regret and fear. We wished we'd never taken that wrong turn. We wished we hadn't walked into the tunnel in the first place.

But now, wishing wouldn't get us out. We knew we had to act, to find a way out or face whatever fate awaited us down here.

So we started digging. With our bare hands, we clawed at the rubble blocking the entrance. Slowly, tiny slivers of daylight began to seep through the cracks. It wasn't much, but it was enough to keep us going.

Then something happened that made the blood run cold.

Kai suddenly froze, his eyes wide as he stared toward the far end of the tunnel. "There's… there's a face," he whispered, trembling so hard his voice shook. It wasn't just any face, it looked like something from a ghost story, pale and haunting.

Even Jimmy, usually the calmest among us, looked shaken. "That's no joke," he said quietly. "It's a ghost… or something like it. They say it comes out at night."

Samantha

Fear pushed us to work faster, digging harder with whatever strength we had left. Our hands scraped and clawed at the earth, desperate to clear a path.

Bit by bit, we made a small hole just big enough to crawl through.

By the time the clock hit around 2 AM, we knew we'd missed check-in. The holiday was gone. But survival, getting out alive, was all that mattered now.

The first light of dawn crept slowly into the tunnel, casting long shadows on the cold, rough walls. We were exhausted, covered in dirt and bruises from hours of digging and crawling through the tight, dark space. The night had felt endless, but finally, the faint sounds of life outside started to reach us, distant voices, footsteps, and the unmistakable sound of dogs barking.

We shouted for help, our voices raw and hoarse, hoping someone would hear us. Minutes felt like hours as we called out again and again, clinging to the hope that we weren't alone.

Then, through the tunnel's gloom, a figure appeared, a young woman walking her dog. The dog, a lively little thing named Pickles, seemed to sense something was wrong and tugged at the leash, leading her closer to our desperate cries.

She stopped, startled at first, then quickly understood the situation. Without hesitation, she pulled out her phone and called for emergency services. The sound of sirens soon filled the air, breaking through the stillness of the early morning.

Rescue workers arrived with tools and determination. They worked swiftly, breaking apart the rubble that had trapped us, freeing us from the tunnel's dark grip. Each step outside into the fresh air felt like a gift, the warmth of the sun on our faces, the wide-open sky, and the sound of life buzzing around us.

Though our holiday was ruined, we were alive, and that was all that mattered.

As we climbed into our cars to head home, the mood was quiet but grateful. We all knew this would be a story to remember, a reminder that sometimes, even the most exciting plans can go horribly wrong.

But we also learned a lesson, never to miss a wrong turn again. And despite everything, we promised ourselves another chance at the Caribbean, another holiday, another time to chase blue skies and clear seas. But this time, with more caution and a little less adventure.

Poppy Field Terror

The morning sun had just begun to rise over the sprawling farm, casting a warm golden glow across the fields. It was early July, the height of summer, and the air carried that familiar mix of fresh earth and morning dew. Tommy, a sturdy 60-year-old rancher, was already up and moving, as he did every day. He made his way toward the milking shed, ready to start the long, familiar routine of preparing the cows. The farm was large, with rolling pastures that stretched as far as the eye could see, alive with the soft sounds of animals waking up.

There were cows lowing patiently, waiting for their morning milking, and chickens bustling about in the henhouse, their eggs steadily piling up. Tommy had always loved the rhythm of farm life, early starts, long days, endless work. From tending crops to attending the occasional birth of a calf, there was never a dull moment, and certainly never a shortage of tasks. The sun could be unforgiving, beating down hard through the summer months, but Tommy didn't mind. This was the life he knew and loved.

One of his favorite spots on the farm was a two-acre poppy field, vibrant with bright red flowers swaying gently in the breeze. Those poppies held a special place in Tommy's heart, they reminded him of the sacrifices of war, a tribute to his father who had fought bravely but never returned home. The sight of those red blooms was a quiet homage to remembrance and respect, something Tommy carried with him every day.

On this particular morning, Tommy had a rare day off. While the rest of his family worked tirelessly to keep the farm running, he decided to take some time for himself. He grabbed a blanket and made his way through the poppy field, feeling the soft petals brush against his hands. Settling down among the tall stalks, he lay back, letting the sun warm his face, the gentle breeze cool his skin. Above him, clouds drifted lazily across the sky, and the sweet songs of birds filled the air. For a brief moment, all the noise of the farm faded away, leaving only the calm of the field and the peaceful rhythm of nature.

Fear The Bloody Forest In The Dark

The peace didn't last long. As Tommy lay there, soaking in the warm sun and listening to the birdsong, a sudden movement caught his attention. Something was crawling over him, a slow, unsettling sensation that sent a chill through his body. His eyes snapped open, and his heart jumped into his throat. There, slithering across his stomach, was a snake.

Not just any snake. Tommy recognized it immediately: a timber snake, sleek and deadly. Its forked tongue flickered in and out, tasting the air, while its cold scales slid against his skin. The snake hissed softly, a chilling warning that froze Tommy in place. Panic threatened to take over, but he forced himself to stay still, knowing that sudden movements could provoke the creature.

Sweat poured down his face as the snake coiled and uncoiled, exploring its new territory, right on him. His mind raced. He couldn't shout for help or move; he was trapped, powerless beneath the weight of fear and the serpent itself. The sun beating down felt less warm now, more like a spotlight on his helplessness. Then, the itching started, uncontrollable sneezes wracked his body, making it even harder to stay calm.

Suddenly, the snake struck, biting deep into his stomach. The sharp pain was immediate, fiery and intense, and Tommy let out a yelp he couldn't hold back. The timber snake quickly slithered away into the tall poppies, leaving Tommy alone, shaking and in serious danger.

Desperation took over. He shouted as loud as he could, hoping someone, anyone, might be nearby. Time felt endless, the distance between him and safety growing with every moment. Then, faintly, he heard footsteps crunching through the field. Relief flooded through him as a passerby appeared, a stranger who quickly called for an ambulance.

Paramedics arrived, rushing Tommy through the fields and into the waiting ambulance. The journey to the hospital was a blur of pain and fear, but also hope. They hooked him up to drips and machines, monitoring his vitals as he fought through the venom's grip. Days turned into a week, slow but steady healing marking his return from the brink.

Through it all, Tommy's thoughts returned again and again to his farm, to his family, and to the poppy fields that had almost been his undoing. What was meant to be a peaceful moment of rest had turned into a terrifying ordeal. But he was alive, and that was everything.

The sun finally shone brightly again over Tommy's farm, casting long warm rays across the fields and the animals he loved so much. Though he was still recovering, his spirit was determined to move forward. The ordeal with the timber snake had shaken him to the core, but it also sparked something new inside, a drive to find a fresh purpose.

Tommy decided to take up golf, something lighter and gentler than the hard work of the farm, a way to keep active but also relax in a different way. Retirement was on the horizon, and he wanted to build a new chapter in his life, one filled with goals and quiet joys.

Yet, no matter how much he looked forward, the memory of that day in the poppy field never left him. The bright red flowers, so beautiful and peaceful, hid dangers beneath their delicate petals, a harsh reminder that life can change in an instant. The snake's attack had been deadly serious, and Tommy knew he was lucky to be alive.

From that day on, he vowed never to lie down in the poppy fields again. Those fields, with their hidden threats, would always hold a mix of beauty and terror in his mind. But Tommy was stronger now, grateful for survival, and ready to face whatever came next.

Fierce Wind

The final chime of the clock at work echoed in my mind as I closed the office door behind me. Today wasn't just any day, it was my last shift before stepping into a new role, a promotion I'd been quietly dreaming about for months. Manager. It sounded good, felt good. Finally, a chance to take the reins, to make things happen instead of just watching from behind a desk.

The spring evening welcomed me like an old friend. The air was thick with warmth, sticky and heavy, as if the earth itself was holding its breath before nightfall. I glanced down at Carrot, my loyal companion, a medium-sized, shaggy mutt with a goofy grin and eyes full of life. I smiled, the kind of smile that comes from pure contentment.

We walked through the park's familiar gates, the crunch of gravel underfoot mingling with the distant splash of water. The lake sat in the center like a shimmering mirror, reflecting the soft orange hues of the setting sun. It stretched wide and calm, dotted here and there with trees that swayed gently despite the lack of breeze. Ducks were usually bobbing around, but tonight, they were nowhere to be seen. Perhaps they were settling in for the night, just like me.

The sky above was painted in pastel pinks, streaked faintly with wisps of clouds that drifted lazily like cotton candy. The whole scene felt peaceful, almost too perfect, like a moment suspended in time.

Carrot bounded ahead eagerly, nose twitching with every new scent, tail wagging like a flag in slow motion. I grabbed his favorite ball from my pocket, the worn rubber sphere that had seen countless throws and catches. "Ready, boy?" I asked, my voice soft with affection.

With a gleeful bark, Carrot darted after the ball as I hurled it across the wide open field. His paws pounded the earth, ears flapping wildly, until he scooped it up and trotted back, eyes bright with joy. We played until the light began to dim, the shadows stretching longer and the park growing quieter.

Time slipped away without notice, the world narrowed to the sound of panting breaths, the rhythm of paws on grass, the warmth of the fading sun on my skin. It was a rare moment of calm before the inevitable rush of new responsibilities, a brief pause in a life that was about to change.

As dusk settled deeper, I called Carrot back, leash in hand. Together, we headed toward the park's exit, neither of us suspecting that the serene night was about to twist into something far darker.

As we neared the park gate, a strange stillness fell over the air. The warmth that had wrapped around us like a comforting blanket seemed to fade, replaced by an eerie chill crawling down my spine. The usual soft rustling of leaves was gone, the birdsong silenced, and even Carrot's playful energy turned to cautious whimpers. He slowed, his body stiffening, teeth lightly chattering as his gaze darted nervously into the gathering shadows.

Then I noticed it, a mist, low and thick, seeping across the ground like a slow-moving fog, curling around the trunks of the trees and twisting between the lampposts. At first, it seemed harmless, almost magical in the fading light. But as I watched, the mist thickened rapidly, swallowing the path ahead until the park's familiar edges blurred and vanished.

My heart quickened. An unsettling sensation prickled at my skin, as if invisible fingers were trailing lightly across my neck and arms. I swallowed hard, trying to shrug off the sudden fear. "It's just fog," I whispered to myself. "Nothing more."

Carrot growled low in his throat, a sound I'd never heard from him before. His body trembled uncontrollably now, and despite the leash in my hand, he pulled toward the trees, ears pinned back. I looked around, the park was deserted, save for us. No other walkers, no distant chatter, no reassuring lights flickering from nearby houses. Just an oppressive silence, broken only by the faint whisper of the wind.

And then it came.

A fierce gust slammed into me from nowhere, cutting through my thin summer dress like a blade of ice. The mist swirled violently, transforming into a swirling, smoky vortex that churned at my feet. I staggered, gripping the leash tighter as Carrot barked frantically, his yelps rising in pitch with the roaring wind.

From within that dark whirlwind, I thought I heard a voice, soft at first, like a hiss carried on the breeze, then growing clearer, sharper, colder: "I will take your soul from the earth…"

The words sliced through me like a knife, igniting every nerve with raw panic. My breaths came fast, shallow. The world tilted. My feet scrambled for purchase on the uneven ground, but the wind whipped and clawed, pressing against me like some malevolent force determined to drag me into the heart of the storm.

Carrot tugged wildly, his body tense and trembling. I tried to call to him, but my voice caught in my throat. The swirling mist blocked the path ahead, and behind us, the park seemed to disappear into shadow. The only thing that was real was the howl of the wind and the dreadful presence lurking within it.

Then, through the swirling chaos, I glimpsed it, a face. Twisted and cruel, with glaring red eyes burning like embers, a nose curled in a grotesque snarl, no ears to speak of. It floated within the storm, grinning at me with a malevolent hunger. The face seemed to feed on my terror, howling its fury in a sound that tore at my sanity.

I staggered backward, desperate for something to hold onto. My fingers found the rough bark of a tree, and I clung to it as the twister tried to rip me free. Carrot barked nonstop, yelping and whining, but there was no one to hear us, no help, no escape.

The night had turned into a nightmare, and I was trapped in its grasp.

The face in the wind howled again, its scream sharp and cruel, echoing through the swirling mist like a banshee's wail. My heart pounded wildly, every nerve screaming for me to run, but the storm held me fast, its icy fingers clawing at my skin, biting through my summer dress and chilling me to the bone.

Samantha

Carrot was barking frantically beside me, his tiny body trembling, but he refused to let go. Somehow, his presence gave me the strength to fight back the rising tide of panic. I gripped the tree tighter, digging my nails into the bark, willing myself to stay grounded, to resist the terrible force that sought to pull me into the darkness.

The wind whipped around us like a living thing, swirling into a twisted tornado that sucked at my feet, threatening to drag me off the earth. The red-eyed face loomed closer, its grin widening, teeth sharp and cruel. It was a nightmare made flesh, a creature born of fear and fury.

And then, just as suddenly as it had come, the wind began to weaken. The swirling mist thinned, the terrible face faded into a shadow, and the storm's roar softened to a distant whisper. The oppressive chill lifted, replaced by the soft pink glow of dawn breaking over the horizon.

I sank to my knees, trembling and soaked with sweat and cold, my breath ragged. Carrot licked my hand, his eyes full of worry but also relief. The nightmare was over.

I didn't speak of that night to anyone. How could I? Who would believe a face in the wind, a voice stealing souls? But every time I walked near that park, especially as night fell, I felt the old fear stir inside me, reminding me that some places hold shadows deeper than the night.

Still, life went on. I embraced my new role as manager with determination, finding comfort in the routines of work and the simple joy of Carrot's company. The fierce wind had tested me, and I had survived.

But I vowed never to walk alone in that park after dark again.

The Puzzle Box of Evil

Autumn had arrived like a breath held too long, exhaled into the cold. The morning air clung to the windows in a delicate mist, blurring the world outside into pale smudges of gold and gray. I opened the blinds slowly, half-awake, and stared out at the bare trees lining the edge of my garden , tall, thin things with twisted limbs, reaching like bony fingers toward a sky that promised no warmth.

Crisp leaves blanketed the ground below, crunching softly beneath the breeze that stirred them like whispers. Everything felt quiet. Still. A little too still.

I stretched, bones aching from another restless night, and padded across the cold wooden floor to the bathroom. The mirror greeted me with tired eyes and a familiar weariness. Just another Saturday, I told myself. Just another day trying to outrun the echo of silence in an empty house.

The shower steamed up the glass quickly, fogging the world again. I stood under the water longer than I should have, letting the heat chase the chill from my skin, pretending it could do the same for whatever was lodged deep in my chest , a weight I couldn't name, but always carried.

I dressed carefully. A thick cardigan, a soft jumper, ankle boots I hadn't worn since last year. The kind of outfit that felt like armor against the wind. I wasn't sure why I felt the need to protect myself, but something in the air pressed gently at the edges of my thoughts. Like a warning I couldn't quite hear.

Outside, the world looked harmless enough. But I couldn't shake the feeling that something , just out of sight , was watching.

By midmorning, the sky had brightened but never quite bloomed. The sun hung low, casting a strange amber hue across the pavement , like it was pretending to be cheerful, but something behind it was rotting. Still, the air was dry and not too cold, and I figured that was enough to tempt me outside.

I met Lily at our usual café on the corner of Pine and Holloway. She was already inside when I arrived, sipping on milky tea and scrolling through her phone. The bell above the door gave its tired little jingle as I stepped in, and she looked up with a grin.

"About time," she teased. "I ordered you the usual."

"Life-saving as always," I said, sliding into the booth across from her. The seat was warm, the coffee hotter. For a while, it felt like normal , two women talking nonsense over caffeine and flaky pastries, pretending we weren't just drifting through time.

We gossiped, laughed, traded the latest scraps of neighborhood drama. The kind of talk that didn't really matter but held you together all the same.

Time slipped past us unnoticed, and soon we were weaving through the narrow side streets of the high street, arms heavy with bags, boots thudding softly on the pavement.

Then Lily paused.

"Hey , look." She pointed to a narrow storefront tucked between a shuttered bookstore and a closed butcher shop. *Greaves & Sons Antiques,* read the sign, its lettering faded and chipped. The display window was cluttered with strange old things , cracked dolls, rusted spoons, tarnished lockets, and… something else.

A box.

Square. Wooden. Carved with symbols I didn't recognize.

"I've never seen this shop open before," Lily said, her voice dropping just slightly.

The door creaked when we stepped inside. The air was stale , not just dusty, but old. It smelled like forgotten things. Time bottled up and left to spoil.

Behind the counter stood a man who looked like he'd been carved from smoke. Thin, gray, silent. His eyes followed us without blinking.

Lily nudged me. "Look," she whispered, pointing to the puzzle box. "That's totally your kind of thing."

She wasn't wrong. I loved puzzles , the more complicated, the better. But something about this one made my skin tighten. It didn't look handmade. It looked… ancient. Designed for something more than fun.

I picked it up. The box was surprisingly warm, pulsing faintly in my palm, like it had a heartbeat.

"How much?" I asked the man.

His voice rasped like dry paper. "Ten pounds."

"Seriously?" Lily blinked. "This looks like it belongs in a museum."

The man didn't respond. Just slid a paper bag across the counter, already opened, waiting.

I hesitated , just for a moment , and then handed him the money.

He dropped the box into the bag. His fingers were ice-cold. As we stepped out into the street again, I glanced back.

The door was already locked.

The sign now read:

Closed. Permanently.

Lily and I stared at it, both of us suddenly quiet.

"That's weird," she muttered. "Like... really weird."

I nodded slowly, fingers tightening around the bag.

The sun was still shining, but the light felt off , like it didn't belong here. Like it was borrowed.

Neither of us said what we were thinking. But we both felt it.

Something had changed the moment I touched that box.

The kettle hissed, steam curling toward the ceiling like fingers reaching for something they couldn't grasp. The scent of ground coffee filled the kitchen, rich and bitter, cutting through the faint unease that had followed us home. Lily sat at the small table by the window, slicing into a cream cake, but her eyes kept drifting to the paper bag on the counter.

Neither of us said it, but the box hadn't left our minds.

I set two mugs down and reached for the bag. It crinkled in my hand, louder than it should have been, like the sound didn't belong in this world.

"You sure it's not cursed or something?" Lily half-laughed, but there was no weight behind it.

I pulled the box out.

Up close, it was even stranger , not just carved, but etched. Tiny, precise grooves covered every inch of the wood. Some looked like symbols, others like tiny gears fused into the grain itself. It was heavier than before. And warmer.

We studied it in silence for a few minutes, turning it slowly in our hands, trying to find where it opened.

Lily leaned closer. "Try this corner. Looks like it moves."

I pressed it.

Click.

We both jumped. The sound was sharp, mechanical, final. Something inside the box shifted. A piece slid open by itself, revealing another, then another, as the cube began unfolding in slow, deliberate movements. Like it had been waiting.

A light , blinding and white-hot , burst from its center. Not glowing. **Beaming.** It lit the room like a lightning strike, casting warped shadows across the ceiling.

And then came the voice.

It wasn't human.

It wasn't even language.

It was a sound that crawled through the air like smoke, low and wet, whispering directly into the back of the skull. Words that made no sense but carried meaning all the same , **You should not have opened me.**

Lily screamed.

She stumbled back, knocking over her chair, coffee spilling like blood across the tiles. Her eyes were wide, glassy. I knew what she was thinking. I was thinking it too.

We had opened something we shouldn't have.

Something that wasn't meant to be touched. A door, a cage, a lock that held something old and angry inside.

The voice echoed again , higher this time, sharper, like metal being pulled through bone.

Lily grabbed her coat. "No. Nope. I can't. Sam, I, I have to go. I'm sorry."

She fled, not even bothering to close the front door behind her.

I stood frozen in the kitchen, the box pulsing faintly in my hands, light still leaking from its seams like blood from a wound.

The air around me felt thicker. Wrong. Like something invisible had stepped into the room and was watching me now , breathing just behind my shoulder.

The box didn't stop unfolding.

And I didn't dare touch it again.

The house was quiet.

Too quiet.

After Lily left, I sat on the sofa for hours, the box pulsing faintly on the table like a dying heart. I didn't touch it again. I couldn't. Eventually, exhaustion dragged me upstairs like a tide I couldn't fight.

I collapsed into bed fully clothed, blanket only half covering me. My body ached, my head was foggy, and the last thing I remember before sleep took me was the light from the hallway blinking out on its own.

Then something changed.

I didn't wake.

I **snapped** awake , like being yanked from beneath water.

I couldn't move.

My arms were stretched wide and tied to the bedposts with something rough , fabric? rope? It bit into my skin. My legs were bound at the ankles, twisted at an angle that made my muscles scream. And worse , my mouth. Gagged. Forced shut by a cloth soaked in something bitter, like rust and rot.

I tried to scream, but it came out a choked gasp, swallowed by the dark.

My eyes darted across the room. Shadows swirled along the walls like oil in water. The air was **wrong** , too cold and too still, like something had turned off the world outside. There were no sounds. No wind. No cars. No time.

And then… they came.

Two shapes peeled themselves from the corners of the room, stepping into the faint light that flickered from nowhere.

They weren't human.

They had **human shapes**, yes , but only like a child's crude imitation of a body. Towering, skeletal. Horns twisted from their foreheads like broken roots. One had thick, matted hair across its back, its face flat and eyeless. It sniffed the air loudly, animal-like, head jerking side to side. The other was smooth-skinned, ash-colored, with long fingers and slit-pupiled eyes that locked on me like I was prey.

I thrashed. Useless.

The ropes didn't budge. The gag held. My heartbeat pounded in my skull, and my skin felt too tight , like it knew what was coming before I did.

The smooth one stepped forward.

It didn't speak. It made no noise.

It only moved over me, knelt on the mattress, and pulled my legs wider with impossible strength.

I screamed into the gag, tears already spilling. It didn't matter.

It was happening.

The creature didn't hesitate. There was no hesitation in monsters.

I felt everything , every motion, every vibration of its inhuman body. It was cold. So cold inside. Like ice and smoke and hate. My wrists bled from the ropes as I pulled against them, but there was no escape. No one coming. Only the other one , the hairy, eyeless one , standing by the bed, breathing me in like it was enjoying the smell of fear.

They didn't speak.

They only **did**.

When it was done, the smooth one rose slowly, something leaking from its skin like black sap. I couldn't stop sobbing , not from pain alone, but from the **knowing**.

It wasn't done with me.

I wasn't just hurt. I was **claimed**.

The creatures turned, melting back into the corners, vanishing like shadows peeled from light.

I lay there, trembling, wrists raw, gag soaked with tears and blood.

The box was still open downstairs.

And somewhere deep inside me, something **shifted**.

Morning came without warning.

Samantha

There was no sunrise , just a faint light leaking into the room, pale and wrong, like it didn't belong to this world. The air was heavy. Still. And the creatures were gone.

I lay there for what felt like hours, trembling, barely breathing, the ropes still cutting deep into my skin. Every limb ached. My body was numb in places I didn't know could go numb.

But I was alive.

And I was alone.

I began to move. Slowly. Painfully. One wrist at a time, I twisted, dug in my nails, tore skin. The ropes were tight, but they were fabric. Old. Frayed. I dug and pulled and bled and **screamed** into the silence until finally, one hand came free.

Then the other.

I collapsed off the side of the bed, my legs still tangled in the bindings. I ripped them off, not caring how much flesh they took with them. My breath came in ragged sobs, and I couldn't stop shaking.

Every step down the stairs felt like walking through molasses. My legs were jelly. My clothes were soaked. My skin still **felt** the cold of that thing inside me.

But I had to finish it.

The box still sat on the table , open, humming faintly. The symbols on its sides were glowing now, slow and pulsing like a heartbeat.

I grabbed it with bare hands, not caring how hot it felt. Not caring if it burned me.

I stumbled into the garden, nearly collapsing on the lawn. I found the old rusted fire pit near the back fence and tossed the box in. It hit the bottom with a metallic thud, like something alive , something angry , didn't want to go.

I struck a match.

The moment the flame touched it, the box screamed.

Fear The Bloody Forest In The Dark

Not a sound from wood.

A sound from something inside.

It shrieked like a trapped animal. The fire exploded upward, towering, twisting. A blast of white-hot light tore into the sky like a signal, or a warning. Or a **release**.

I covered my ears and dropped to my knees.

The air around the fire shimmered , warping, vibrating, **breaking** , and I could feel the scream *inside* my bones. It didn't fade. It didn't die. It **melted** down into a whisper that would never leave.

The fire died on its own.

The box was gone.

But the horror wasn't.

Days passed.

I didn't leave the house. I barely slept. I threw out the bedsheets. Scrubbed every inch of the room. Showered until my skin peeled.

It didn't matter.

The silence remained.

Then came the sickness.

At first I blamed stress , the dizziness, the nausea, the weight pressing low in my stomach. But when the days turned to weeks and the sickness didn't stop, I took the test.

I knew the answer before I saw it.

Pregnant.

Not from any man.

Not from any world I understood.

I stared at the result for a long time. I didn't cry. I didn't scream. I just sat there, hollowed out. A puppet in someone else's nightmare.

I tried to get help. Doctors. Clinics. Friends.

Samantha

No one believed me.

Of course they didn't.

How do you explain something like this?

"I was raped by something that doesn't have a name."

They looked at me like I was crazy. Offered pamphlets. Soft voices. Pity.

No one could help me.

And by the time I found someone who might, it was too late to undo it.

The thing growing inside me wasn't human. I felt it move long before I should have. It didn't kick , it twisted. It curled. It *watched* me from the inside.

I gave birth alone.

It was small. Deformed. Its eyes too large, its fingers too long. It didn't cry. It just stared at me , silently, knowingly , for hours before its body gave out.

I buried it in the woods behind the garden.

I didn't give it a name.

I didn't want to.

It's been months now. The old man from the antique shop? Gone. The building was gutted. Empty. Like he'd never existed. Like the shop was never really **there**.

People talk to me differently now , like I'm glass. Like I'm not whole anymore.

And maybe they're right.

But I survived.

Barely.

And I've learned something I'll never forget:

Fear The Bloody Forest In The Dark

Some boxes aren't meant to be opened.

Some puzzles don't want to be solved.

And some doors, once unlocked, **don't ever close.**

Homeless Drug Addiction Horror Story

The sun was brutal. Not warm, merciless. It baked the cracked pavement until it peeled, burned into my skin like it hated me. The sky was blue, wide open, watching. No clouds. No shade. Just heat and silence.

My name is Leah. I'm Chinese. Twenty-three years old. And I live on the streets of Phoenix, Arizona.

I've got nothing but the clothes on my back, threadbare jeans, a faded hoodie, and shoes worn flat from walking nowhere. No clean change. No toothbrush. No bag. No money. Just me, moving through the dust.

Every day's the same: beg, smoke, fix, survive.

I smile a lot. People like it better when you smile. They think it means you're okay. I'll puff a cigarette and wave at strangers. Most keep walking. Some stop. I don't ask for much, just a dollar. Enough to get a drink. Maybe a smoke. Maybe something stronger if I'm lucky.

The streets are loud but empty. Dirty but quiet. They're my home. The corners I curl up in at night. The broken concrete I rest on when the heat gets too much. No roof. No comfort. Just a city full of things I can't have.

I don't feel scared. I feel... nothing, mostly.

The drugs help with that. Keep my mind from thinking too much. Alcohol smooths the edges. Just enough to stay numb, just enough to forget the hunger in my stomach and the ache in my bones.

I don't clean my teeth. I don't brush my hair. There's no point. I don't have a mirror anyway. What would I be fixing? I look how I feel, scratched out, like the edge of a used coin. Dirty clothes. Dirty hands. Dirty world.

I used to imagine what a normal life would be like. Now, I don't bother. This is normal now. This is the version of me the sun sees every day.

Fear The Bloody Forest In The Dark

And it doesn't look away.

The sun came back just like it always does, too soon, too strong.

I rolled over on the concrete, my cheek stuck to the warm pavement. My neck ached. My back was stiff. The heat was already climbing before I'd even opened my eyes.

Another day.

Same story.

I pulled myself upright, blinking against the brightness. I needed shade. A patch of wall, the edge of a dumpster, even the back steps of a shuttered shop. Just somewhere to sit where the sun wouldn't eat me alive.

I lit a cigarette with shaky hands. Half the tobacco had already crumbled out the side. Didn't matter. I smoked it anyway.

A few hours passed in blurs, faces, footsteps, voices talking at me, around me. I held out my hand now and then, smiled if someone made eye contact. Asked for a dollar. Never more. Never greedy.

I knew how to make it work.

I walked a little. Sat a little. Took another drag. Watched the same cars go by like they were stuck in a loop.

There's no point brushing your teeth when you don't eat much. No point combing your hair when there's nothing left to impress. I'd stopped caring a long time ago. The mirror in the gas station bathroom showed a stranger, skin dull, lips cracked, eyes sunken and still. That was fine. I didn't need to know her anymore.

My fix was all I needed.

Something small to keep the noise down. Just enough to stop the shaking in my hands, the itch under my skin. My body needed it. My mind begged for it.

It was the only thing that made the world feel quiet.

Samantha

No family. No one coming. No number to call. Just me and the rhythm of the street, wake up, walk, smoke, beg, score, sleep. Repeat.

People think it's chaos. But it isn't. It's a pattern. A slow unraveling. Like pulling one thread over and over until you disappear.

And I was disappearing.

Not all at once.

Just a little more every day.

I scored something different that day.

A stronger fix. Not the usual, something deeper, heavier, meaner. I didn't ask questions. When you're desperate, you take what's handed to you. I walked until I found a quiet patch of shade behind a boarded-up liquor store, sat down, and unwrapped it carefully, like it might shatter.

The foil glinted in the sun. My hands moved without thinking.

I took the hit.

Within minutes, my body started to go.

First it was the silence. Not peace, just everything muting all at once. Then the weight. Like my bones turned to lead and the air turned thick, too thick to breathe. My arms wouldn't move. My head slumped forward. I couldn't lift it.

I was a puppet with the strings cut.

The world narrowed to a small, flickering tunnel. Sound came and went like static. Somewhere, I could hear voices. Distant. Then closer. A crowd maybe. People standing over me. But they didn't feel real.

I couldn't look up.

Couldn't speak.

Couldn't move.

Then the sirens.

Screaming in the heat like they were angry at me. I wanted to scream too, but my mouth didn't work. Everything felt far away. Too far. My body didn't belong to me anymore.

I was dying.

And I couldn't even feel afraid.

The next thing I knew, there were bright lights over my face. White tile ceiling. Cold air. Machines beeping near my ears. I was in a hospital, Phoenix General, probably. Someone said my name. A nurse, maybe. Someone else held my wrist, checking for a pulse that wasn't sure if it wanted to come back.

The drug had moved through me. I was still high, but it was thinner now. Worn down by oxygen and IV fluids and strangers' hands trying to keep me here.

I didn't thank them.

I didn't cry.

I just stared at the ceiling, waiting to be allowed to leave.

Eventually they let me go. No follow-up. No one to call. No questions beyond the paperwork.

Just back out into the sun.

Back to the street that had waited for me all along.

They gave me paper shoes and a clear plastic bag for my clothes. That was it. No ride. No plan. Just a nod from the discharge nurse and the door sliding shut behind me with a soft mechanical hiss.

I was still groggy. My body felt hollowed out, stretched thin by whatever had nearly stopped my heart. But my legs worked, and that was enough. I started walking again.

The city was just as I left it.

Phoenix didn't notice I'd been gone. The streets didn't care.

The sun was already climbing high. I lit a cigarette from the crumpled pack someone had dropped near the hospital entrance and walked with my hand out, same as always. Begging, not bothering to explain. Most didn't stop. A few did. Loose change. A nod. A wordless transaction.

Eventually, I had thirty dollars folded tight in my pocket.

Enough.

I found a burger place, paid in cash, ate it slow, each bite heavy but hollow, like chewing paper. I washed it down with soda, bought a pack of smokes at the corner mart, then headed back toward the strip where the fixers moved in shadows.

I didn't have a bag. No purse. Nothing to carry things in. I kept the foil in my sleeve. Warm from the sun. Familiar from use. The edges were burnt and folded, blackened like the inside of my lungs.

People noticed. They always noticed.

They saw the way I held it. The way my fingers shook a little when I lit it. The way I disappeared behind my eyes when I inhaled. But no one said anything.

Not anymore.

The drug crawled through me like a whisper. My muscles uncoiled. My thoughts slowed to a syrupy hum. I melted against the side of a building, watching the sidewalk flicker in and out of focus.

This was the only thing that made sense.

Not the hospital.

Not the people with their clean clothes and unbroken routines.

Just this.

Fix. Drift. Fade. Repeat.

That overdose hadn't scared me straight.

It had just proven what I already knew.

You can be saved once.

But it doesn't mean you'll stay that way.

Fear The Bloody Forest In The Dark

The streets don't change.

Not really.

The names on the storefronts might fade, the traffic lights might glitch, but the bones of this place stay the same. Concrete. Smoke. Silence.

This part of Phoenix, this hood, it isn't alive. It doesn't breathe. It just waits. Swallows people whole. Lets them rot in slow motion.

I walk these roads in rags. Jeans split at the knees. Shirt stained and stretched from too many days without washing. Shoes flapping open at the soles. I pass piles of trash, bent needles, empty bottles, the shadows of people who used to have names.

No one looks up anymore.

No one looks clean.

I see them, the others. Slumped in doorways. Faces twitching, mouths moving with no sound. I call them drugged zombies, but I'm no different. We all sit with the same ghosts. Wait for the same poison to slide through our veins and shut out the noise.

This is what hell looks like.

Not fire. Not punishment.

Just a dirty street under a sky that never rains.

People tell you to get help. As if help is something you can afford. I don't have insurance. I don't have an ID. I don't even have a real name anymore. Just "hey" or "you" or "move along."

Rehab costs more than I've seen in a year. Detox is for people with someone waiting for them on the other side.

I've got no one.

No address.

No way out.

Samantha

So I hustle. I scrounge. I play the same game every day, smile, ask, survive. Just enough dollars for a fix. Just enough high to get through another stretch of hours.

The street is filthy. The air burns. But it's familiar.

And after a while, familiar is safer than change.

I don't even remember what I looked like before this. Before the smoke. Before the foil. Before the quiet took over.

I just keep walking.

Another corner.

Another day.

The cycle doesn't stop.

And maybe I don't want it to.

The Moon That Changed into an Alien

The clock read 5:11 AM when I finally stepped out of the office. Phoenix was still dark, the sky caught between night and morning, but the air carried no coolness, just the stale breath of concrete and fatigue. I stretched my neck, rubbed my eyes, and walked. No car. No ride. Just the pavement and my shadow under the occasional flicker of a streetlamp.

I own the firm, immigration law, court appearances, endless paperwork, and clients always on the verge of losing something precious. Owning the business meant everything fell on me. Long hours. Little rest. No space to breathe. Tonight, well, this morning, marked the last day before a two-week break. Ramadan was coming, and with it, a pause. A reset. I needed both.

By the time I reached home, dawn threatened the edge of the sky. I kicked off my shoes, stepped straight into the shower. Warm water helped shake off the courtroom echoes, the fluorescent lighting, the smell of stale coffee and ink. I dried off, changed into loose cotton clothes, and went straight to the kitchen.

Dinner, or breakfast, depending on how you count time, was simple: rice, cauliflower, and halal chicken cooked the way my mother used to make it. Aloo gobi. My favorite. I placed the plate in front of me, murmured "Mashallah," and took the first bite in silence. The flavors grounded me, turmeric, cumin, heat. Familiar. Nourishing. Clean.

Afterward, I laid out my prayer mat and faced the qibla. My body ached, but my spirit softened. I prayed quietly, not asking for much, just rest. Peace. A moment of stillness. I thanked Allah for bringing me this far.

When I finished, I stepped out into the garden. The silence was profound. No cars, no footsteps, not even the hiss of wind. The neighborhood seemed frozen. I sat down on the old iron bench beneath the cypress tree, wrapped a thin shawl around my shoulders, and exhaled.

Samantha

Above me, the sky looked unusually still. No clouds. No stars. Just a waiting blackness, and the moon.

Full. Bright. Watching.

The stillness felt too complete.

I leaned back on the bench, eyes lifted toward the sky. The moon hung low and bright, unnaturally so. Not golden, not pale, but almost white-blue, humming with a kind of intensity I couldn't name. I blinked, expecting it to dull. It didn't.

A breeze brushed across my skin. Sharp. Not cold, sharp. Like air moving too fast, slicing instead of cooling. I wrapped the shawl tighter. The hair on my arms stood up, and something in my chest tightened.

I looked up again.

The moon had changed.

It was no longer round.

Its edges warped, forming ridges and shapes that didn't belong in the sky. A strange hue began to spread across it, greenish, slick, as if something beneath the surface was pressing outward, trying to come through.

And then, eyes.

Not imagined. Not metaphor.

Eyes.

Two black ovals, glossy and deep, blinked into existence near the center of the moon's face. They moved. Looked. Focused.

On me.

My lips parted, but no sound came. My fingers gripped the edge of the bench.

I whispered the only thing I could: "Bismillah."

Still, the fear did not pass.

The eyes turned red.

Fear The Bloody Forest In The Dark

A long, twisted grin spread beneath them, inhuman, crooked, too wide. The face was no longer a trick of shadow. It was sculpted into the moon's surface, peering down like a god or a predator. Watching. Smiling.

I whispered again, "Allah Akbar… Allah Akbar…"

But the words felt too small, too soft to compete with the weight of that thing in the sky.

My body froze. The breeze became a gale. Wind howled down from nowhere, circling the garden, lifting dust and leaves and the edges of my shawl.

The moonface grinned wider.

Its eyes pulsed.

My prayers came faster, inside my head, nearly panicked.

It wasn't the moon anymore.

It was something else.

And it had come for me.

I tried to move.

Tried to stand, to run, to retreat into the safety of my home, just a few steps away. But my body didn't listen. My knees buckled before I could rise. I collapsed onto the wet grass, palms sinking into the soil, breath ragged.

The wind howled louder, slashing across my skin. The moon , or whatever it had become , loomed above, larger than before. Its eyes glowed like coals. That grin hadn't faded. It had widened.

I was being watched.

Not like a person watches a person.

Like a hunter watches prey.

"Bismillah," I whispered, the word dry on my tongue. "Bismillah…"

Samantha

But even as I prayed, my arms went numb. A weight pressed down on my chest, invisible but heavy. My legs twitched, then froze. I couldn't sit up. Couldn't lift my head. Something was inside me, locking the joints, silencing the nerves.

I was awake. Aware. And entirely trapped.

The sky didn't move. No stars blinked. Just that monstrous face in the moon, watching with red eyes full of joyless hunger.

I opened my mouth to scream.

Nothing came out.

Not even a gasp.

Then it began to spit.

A thick stream of something black-red and viscous slid from its mouth , not like rain, but heavier, purposeful. It splattered across my chest, my face, my arms. Sticky. Warm. Reeking of metal and rot.

I wanted to scream again. I couldn't.

I tried to close my eyes. They wouldn't shut.

My heart beat against a cage of stillness. My breath came in shallow jolts.

The blood soaked through my shawl, my clothes, down to my skin. I was drenched. Drenched in something that should not exist.

"Allah…" I tried to whisper. "Ya Allah… keep me safe…"

The words were just thoughts now. Prayers without a voice.

The moon didn't move.

It just watched me from above, grinning, as if pleased that I could do nothing but lie there beneath it , helpless, silent, and slowly unraveling.

And the night did not end.

I don't know how long I lay there , soaked in blood, paralyzed under the eyes of something that wore the moon like a mask.

Fear The Bloody Forest In The Dark

Then came the light.

It split the sky in silence , not a flash, not a beam, but a perfect column of blinding white. It came down like judgment, landing not far from where I lay. The garden lit up like midday. Every blade of grass, every wet leaf, every shadow burned away.

From within that light, a shape descended.

A disc. Metallic, smooth, humming without sound. A craft , not from here. Not from this world. I couldn't believe what I was seeing, and yet I couldn't look away.

A panel opened. A ramp extended, slow and mechanical, until it kissed the earth. Then came the figures.

Two of them.

Tall, green-skinned. Their limbs were too long. Their eyes glowed the same red as the moon. No mouths. Just the sound , a low vibration that passed through the air like thunder buried under the skin.

They walked toward me, slow and precise.

I wanted to scream.

I wanted to run.

But I still couldn't move.

They reached me. Lifted me like I weighed nothing. My body hung limp between them, head rolling to one side. I could see the moon's face again , still smiling above the house I once called mine.

The ship swallowed me in silence.

Inside, the light changed , cool blue, endless corridors of smooth, seamless walls. The air was thick and still. Everything felt muffled, like I'd stepped out of sound itself.

They carried me into a small room. Sterile. Bright. A single bed in the center , metallic, curved. They placed me on it. Strapped my wrists, ankles, forehead, chest. Tight, but I couldn't have moved anyway.

Then they stepped back.

Samantha

And the ship lifted.

I felt it in my bones. A sudden drop in gravity. My stomach twisted. My ears rang. I saw the earth tilt through a curved window , the neighborhood shrinking, then the city, then nothing but black.

I was leaving.

My home.

My firm.

My family.

Ramadan.

All of it was gone, slipping into darkness below me, and I didn't know if I would ever return.

In that moment, I believed this was the end of everything I was.

And no one on earth would know where to look.

They told me I was gone for twenty days.

Twenty.

I don't remember them.

Not in order. Not clearly. Just flashes. Cold metal. Buzzing lights. My body floating in something too thick to be air. Sometimes I heard them , not speaking, but humming, like electricity tuned into thought.

I don't know if I slept. I don't know if they fed me. I know my body didn't feel like my own.

I know I didn't see the sun.

Back home, they searched for me. My family. My coworkers. Neighbors. The police asked questions. They called hospitals. Checked morgues. Looked at security footage. Nothing. I was gone. Vanished from my own garden under a sky no one else thought to question.

Ramadan came and went.

Fear The Bloody Forest In The Dark

They gathered without me.

Broke fast without me.

Prayed without me.

No one knew that I had been taken , stripped of time, stripped of earth. No one knew that I was alive, floating somewhere in a sky too dark to name.

And then, one day, I woke up.

In my bed.

In my house.

Dry clothes.

No wounds.

No signs.

Just silence.

The garden was empty.

The moon was gone.

My phone showed missed calls, unopened messages. My fridge was still full. The prayer mat lay folded by the door, right where I'd left it. But the weight in my chest told me something permanent had been undone.

I had no answers to give them.

Only a story no one wanted to believe.

And a sense that some part of me hadn't come back.

They didn't interrupt. They didn't laugh. They just stared , silent, wide-eyed, mouths slightly parted as I told them where I'd been, what I'd seen. The moon that wasn't a moon. The face. The storm. The blood. The ship.

Some believed me. Most didn't.

Samantha

They said I was exhausted. Delirious. Suffering from burnout or trauma or maybe a fugue state. They spoke gently, the way you speak to someone whose mind is broken and fragile.

But I knew the truth.

And the truth didn't care whether they believed it.

I tried to go back to work. I answered emails. I sat in the office, hands on the keyboard, staring at forms and case files that once meant everything. I smiled for clients. I walked through motions.

But inside, I was still there.

Still floating.

Still strapped down in a bed I couldn't move from, under a face I couldn't unsee.

The nightmares came soon after.

They started slow , shadows in dreams, flashes of green and red. Then came the grinning face. Always above me. Always watching. The moon, warped and full of teeth. Eyes glowing. Laughing without sound.

I'd wake drenched in sweat. Screaming into the dark.

I began leaving the lights on at night. I kept the curtains drawn. The garden, once a place of peace, now felt like a trapdoor. I didn't sit out there anymore. I couldn't.

I prayed harder. I prayed longer. I asked Allah to protect me, to silence the visions, to give me back the time I'd lost.

But it wasn't time I'd lost.

It was safety.

It was certainty.

It was the feeling that the sky above me was just sky, and not something that watched, and waited.

Now, even on clear nights, I don't look up.

Fear The Bloody Forest In The Dark

I don't trust what I'll see.

Because the last time I did, the moon was not a moon.

It was a face.

Grinning down at me.

Samantha

The House That Burns You Alive

Night had just fallen, the sky dusk settling softly over the earth. It was a warm summer's night, and I lay in bed with my dog, Sniper, a fluffy white bundle of energy who loved nothing more than cuddles and his nightly treat. Before sleep, I always gave him a little something to help him relax, because he could get jumpy so easily.

Hours slipped by in silence. I woke at dawn, around six in the morning, the sky bright with warm sunshine spilling through the window. As I stretched, a thought came to me, a long country walk, just me and Sniper. He would be so happy out there, roaming the open air.

I got up, took a shower, dressed, and made myself breakfast. Sniper wagged his tail eagerly as I fed him. I packed food for the day ahead, filled a cooler bag with drinks, grabbed a blanket, and packed a bowl for Sniper's water. I clipped on his lead, knowing it was going to be a long, hot day.

With just the two of us, I locked the front door behind me, slid into my car, and started the engine. The road was quiet, mostly back roads leading out toward the countryside. Hours passed as we drove, the scenery slowly unfolding beyond the windows.

At one point, I stopped at a local shop, grabbed some tasty treats for myself, dog treats for Sniper, and filled up the tank. Then we were off again.

Finally, after several more hours, we arrived at the valley. The carpark was empty except for us. Around us, green hills rose sharply, enclosing a deep, silent valley.

I opened the back door, and Sniper leapt out, panting and wagging his tail eagerly. I clipped the lead on and locked the car, carrying the food and blanket as we approached the gate, it was free to enter.

The valley was so still, so silent, I could have shouted and heard the echoes ring back. I laughed quietly to myself at the thought.

Cows and sheep grazed quietly in the distance, their peaceful munching barely disturbing the heavy air. The valley grew darker and denser as we followed the footpath deeper inside. The sun still shone, but the world around us felt still and misty. I didn't mind. It was Sniper's day, and nothing mattered more than his happiness outdoors.

After hours of walking, Sniper and I needed a rest. We settled down on the grass. I opened the lunchbox and poured water into Sniper's bowl. He drank eagerly, panting from the heat, then rolled happily in the soft grass as I ate my lunch. The valley remained quiet and peaceful, the cows and sheep continued grazing, unbothered by our presence.

After a while, we packed up and continued on our walk. As I moved forward, a pressing need forced me to stop, I needed to pee. That's when I stumbled upon something unexpected.

An old, creepy house stood ahead, its broken windows staring out like empty eyes. It was clear no one lived there. Despite the curiosity tugging at me, I kept moving, but Sniper's behavior changed. He pulled sharply on the lead and began to growl, a deep warning rumble that told me he sensed danger nearby.

Reluctantly, I found a spot behind the house to relieve myself. As I did, a strange sound carried through the air, someone yelling, or something like it. The sky darkened quickly, faster than I expected. I had no torch, only the faint light of the night sky and the blanket I carried to keep warm.

The noise unsettled me, but I cautiously looked toward the house again. I didn't go inside, but from what I could see, the place was a charred ruin. Melted flesh seemed to cling to the walls; the inside was burned and blackened beyond recognition. Something about it felt deeply wrong.

Despite the eerie atmosphere, I continued to explore around the house, but nothing else happened. The valley remained silent, and the strange sounds faded away.

Samantha

Eventually, exhaustion took hold. Sniper and I laid down to rest, drifting into sleep under the watchful silence of the valley.

Suddenly, we were awakened by a noise. Flames roared inside the creepy house, bright, intense fire that seemed to burn with a life of its own. The heat pressed against me like a living thing, fierce and overwhelming, even though the house had already been charred beyond belief.

Then, as quickly as it had started, the fire stopped.

In the flickering shadows, I saw a pair of eyes, unmistakably not human. They glowed with cruel laughter and wild yelling.

"I'm dying! I'm the devil! I live in this burned-out house!" The voice echoed, twisted and chilling. "Do not enter this house of evil. You will die if you do."

Fear gripped me, shaking me to my core. The words haunted the air long after they were spoken.

Suddenly, Sniper ran off into the darkness. I was alone, far from the car, with no phone or service to call for help.

I realized then: this was the devil's secret house, a story I had never heard before but now witnessed in terrifying reality.

The fire was hell itself, and I couldn't escape.

I tried to run, but the devil's magic powers forced me back. I was trapped in shock, his evil words swirling in my mind.

"You will die. Blood will be drawn. I am the devil who lives hidden in the unknown. I control and curse."

His power was overwhelming. I was under his spell, bound by invisible ropes I could not see.

Morning came, and with it, the devil vanished.

I was left alone, but still tied up.

I struggled until I freed myself.

The house was pure evil, quiet, waiting, a place in the valley of hell.

Sand Monster

The day was scorching, humid, and still. The air hung dry, not a single breeze stirred the desert's vast silence. I traveled through Morocco's endless sands, riding a camel under the watchful eye of a tour guide. We were bound to spend a few nights in this harsh wilderness, and despite the heat, there was a thrill in the adventure.

Above us, the sky stretched wide and clear, a perfect blue canvas without a single cloud. The sun blazed down mercilessly, making the sand sparkle like broken glass scattered across the dunes. These massive hills of sand rolled on for miles, their peaks glowing bright under the fading light.

The sun began its slow descent, dusk creeping over the horizon, but our journey was far from over. We still had to press deeper into the desert's heart. The heat was relentless, forcing us to pause often, resting wherever we could find a moment's shade or relief.

As the last light slipped away, the sky darkened, and the heat grew thick, almost suffocating. A sudden breeze stirred the sand, a small wind carrying dust and warning. The air grew heavy, thickening with the promise of something darker. I felt it then, a storm was coming.

It arrived fast and fierce.

Despite the warning, we pushed on, moving through the swirling sand until we spotted shelter ahead. A barn stood beside a house, offering refuge from the raging elements. We hurried toward safety as the storm unleashed its fury, sand whipped wildly through the air, rain pelted down, and lightning cracked violently over the dunes.

We had made it just in time.

After finally reaching the shelter, we decided to get some rest. The storm raged outside, the sand whipping relentlessly, the rain pounding the roof, and lightning flashing across the dark sky. Inside, the house and the barn offered a fragile sanctuary for us and the camels.

Samantha

But hours later, a strange noise shattered the uneasy calm. Something was circling the house and barn, moving with an angry, restless energy. The sound was impossible to ignore, like claws scraping and desperate scratching against the door.

We had no communication with the outside world. Out here, survival depended entirely on this shelter.

At first, we tried to ignore the noise, but it only grew louder and more intense. Then came the scratching, frantic and wild, like a lunatic trapped on the other side.

Through the darkness, we caught a glimpse of something, white fangs flashing, a mass of hair shifting in the shadows. The creature was tall, towering like a bear, filled with rage and aggression. Its presence was terrifying.

Trapped in the desert, alone with this huge, terrifying beast, fear took hold. The night stretched on, the storm refusing to settle, and the creature stayed by the door, its massive claws scraping relentlessly against the wood.

We bolted the door and huddled together, trembling in our beds. The terror was overwhelming, and every minute felt endless.

The hours dragged on, heavy and silent, with no sign of daylight. The creature remained outside, blocking our only way out. Its eyes glowed a deep, terrifying red, as if filled with blood itself. Blood dripped from its mouth in slow, dark droplets. It did not speak; it was something entirely other, four-legged, with massive ears that twitched in the darkness and razor-sharp claws that scraped the door with relentless fury.

There was no hope. No chance to escape alive.

The night pressed closer, inching toward dawn, and a faint pink glow began to bleed over the horizon. But the creature remained, a dark shadow against the fading light, its hunger palpable in the heavy air.

Then, as suddenly as it had appeared, the storm ceased. The rain stopped falling, the thunder faded into silence, and the wild sand calmed to a damp, heavy mush beneath our feet.

The creature vanished without a trace, as if swallowed by the desert itself.

Seizing the moment, we hurriedly gathered our belongings and mounted our camels. The sand beneath us was wet and soft, muffling our passage as we rode swiftly over the dunes.

The sun climbed higher, burning hot and bright once again, the sky a flawless blue. Civilization lay ahead, beckoning us from the endless expanse of sand.

Though we had survived the night, the memory of that monstrous presence lingered, a dark stain on our minds. We were shaken to our core by the terror of what had lurked in the desert storm.

No one was hurt, but the fear remained, a silent warning.

We never returned.

The desert still holds its secrets, and somewhere in those vast sand dunes, something waits.

Samantha

The Sky of Hell Turns

The evening air hung heavy and thick, a scorching heat that clung to my skin like a suffocating blanket. The sun was sinking low, casting the sky in a mesmerizing swirl of colors, burning orange bleeding into soft pinks, and shadows of dark grey creeping along the horizon like a slow-moving storm. There wasn't a breath of wind to stir the heavy stillness; the world seemed to pause, trapped in the relentless heat.

My friend and I sat quietly in the garden, just having finished our evening meal. We wanted to savor the last moments of the day, watching as the sun melted behind the skyline and the sky transformed into a living canvas. The earth beneath us radiated warmth, the kind that pressed into your bones and made the very air feel thick and hard to breathe.

After some time, the heat became unbearable, and we decided to take a dip in the pool to cool off. The water was a sudden relief, crisp and refreshing against our overheated skin. We swam lazily for nearly an hour, the coolness washing away the suffocating heat and dulling the sharp edges of the day. Eventually, we climbed out, dripping and laughing softly, drying ourselves with towels before slipping into soft robes.

We settled back outside with glasses of water filled with ice cubes, the only drink we had that night, no alcohol, just cold water to soothe the burning heat lingering on our tongues. The garden felt peaceful again, the only sounds the gentle rustling of leaves and distant insects beginning their nightly chorus.

Then, without warning, the clouds overhead shifted. What had been soft shades of grey deepened to an ominous red, as if the sky itself had been stained with blood. The color spread rapidly, engulfing the sunset in a fiery glow that pulsed and shimmered like a living thing. My chest tightened, a cold knot of unease twisting inside me. I felt it, a creeping dread, a strange energy hanging in the air that I couldn't explain.

Despite the growing fear clawing at my mind, I forced myself to keep watching. The sky glowed brighter, a deep, angry red that seemed to burn its way across the heavens. It wasn't just color anymore; it was a warning, a sign of something dark and terrible.

I turned to my friend, my voice barely a whisper. "What the hell is going on? The sky… it looks like it's covered in blood."

We both stared in silent horror, unable to tear our eyes away from the unfolding nightmare. The beauty of the sunset was gone, replaced by a sinister blood-red shroud that spread across the sky, draping the world below in an unnatural, terrifying light.

We didn't wait long before the fear grew too much to bear. The air shifted suddenly, a sharp, unnatural sound cut through the heavy silence. We rushed inside, slamming the door behind us, desperate for safety from whatever was lurking outside.

But safety was an illusion.

The garden, once peaceful, had transformed into a scene from a nightmare. The sky seemed to explode, bursting down in a crimson deluge that soaked the grass beneath our feet. I stood frozen, staring at the horror before me. "It's blood," I whispered to my friend, voice trembling with disbelief and terror.

Then came the knock.

Slow, deliberate, and chilling.

We peered through the window, no one. But the presence was there, unseen yet unmistakable. A growl rumbled from the shadows, low and menacing. Teeth chattered with a sound like razor blades scraping together. The darkness outside felt alive, pressing against the walls of our home.

We were trapped.

No phone, no mobile service, no way to call for help. The only thing between us and whatever prowled the night was the thin barrier of the door.

The creature in the sky was evil, pure and raw. It didn't want to be disturbed. It hated sound. Every noise we made seemed to provoke it further, making the growls deeper, the scratching louder.

We had to stay still. Stay quiet.

Hours dragged by with the creature's chilling laughter echoing through the night. It was a sound that clawed at our sanity, wild and uncontrollable.

Then, from the shadows, I saw its eyes.

Glowing green, fierce and unnatural.

Its face was twisted, lacking form, and terrifying in its very incompleteness.

A single eye stared back at me, burning with a sinister light.

Horns curled from its head, sharp and black as the night.

Its body was huge, covered in thick, dark hair, like a bear but twisted, monstrous, something born of nightmare.

It roared, a sound so loud and raw it seemed to shake the very sky, turning it blood red as it bled over our garden.

The creature was here.

And it was hungry.

We knew we had to find a way to end this nightmare. The creature had no name, so we called it the Devil Horned Creature, an evil presence we could barely comprehend but deeply feared. It was cursed, a darkness that thrived in the shadows and shrank away from the light.

We discovered its one weakness: daylight.

The demon could not survive in the sun's harsh glare. It hated the brightness, the life-giving warmth that chased it back into darkness. So, we devised a plan, we would keep a light burning through the night, a beacon of hope and protection against the evil that stalked us.

But the demon was relentless.

Fear The Bloody Forest In The Dark

It returned with a fury, roaring, screaming, screeching, a terrible, burning force unleashed in our garden. Flames licked the night air, hungry and fierce, consuming everything in their path. The sky itself seemed aflame, the blood-red light pouring down like a curse.

We fought back with everything we had, the light our only shield against the darkness. Slowly, painstakingly, we managed to drive the creature away, banishing it from our property, breaking its hold on us.

Yet the memories remained, etched deep into our minds. The terror of that night, the garden turned hellscape, the sky stained with blood, the presence of a creature unlike any other, haunted us still.

Even now, the fear lingers, a shadow that never quite fades.

We survived.

But we are forever marked by that night.

The sky was red, and evil walked our garden soil.

Holy Ramadan Quran Story

Ramadan had arrived, the holy month. A time for fasting, prayers, and the gathering of families and communities. The streets buzzed with excitement, as families prepared for the sacred month of reflection. The atmosphere was thick with anticipation, the kind that wraps you up and pulls you into the rhythm of the season. People moved about in their usual hustle, but today there was something different in the air. The city felt alive, pulsing with an energy that only Ramadan could bring.

Shops were stacked high with sweets and delicacies, while food stalls lined the streets, spilling the tempting smells of spiced meats and fresh bread into the air. The sun beat down on the crowded market, where shoppers milled around in long lines. People were eager to fill their stomachs before the dawn of fasting. Everywhere, the mood was festive, as the city came together in unity for the holiday.

Yet, in the shadow of the celebrations, there was a stark reminder of the world beyond. The poor, those with hollow eyes and ragged clothes, moved through the crowd, their cries drowned by the hum of the holiday. A woman with no arms hobbled on crutches, her eyes searching for food, while a child with no legs dragged his body across the cobblestones, his face a picture of hunger. It was a sight that should not have been in the midst of such a sacred time. Yet, there they were, forgotten by the bustling world around them.

As I walked past the butcher's shop, the smell of raw meat hit me, sharp and metallic. Blood stained the pavement, a river of crimson trickling down from the open door. The slaughtered animals hung like trophies, lifeless and grotesque. The meat was being given away, but I couldn't shake the disturbing feeling in my stomach. Something felt off, something that twisted the air with a chill. The whole scene, the slaughter, the blood, the stench, didn't seem to belong to this holy moment.

The mosque stood just around the corner. I could feel the weight of it in the air, heavy with the prayers of those gathered within. But as I walked past, a shiver ran through me. It wasn't a normal feeling, something was wrong. A deep sense of foreboding settled in my chest, making my steps slow. The street was filled with people, all heading to the mosque for the evening prayers, the ritualistic gathering that marked the first night of Ramadan. But I couldn't shake the sense that something terrible was about to unfold. The energy in the air had shifted.

I knew that I should stay clear of the mosque, that it would be crowded, filled with too many people. But more than that, I couldn't bring myself to walk any closer. It was as if an invisible force was warning me away. I needed to leave, to get away from it all. The hairs on the back of my neck stood up, a primal instinct telling me that this day, this Ramadan, was not going to be like the rest.

The peace that hung in the air shattered with a sudden, deafening bang. The world seemed to tilt, the ground shaking beneath my feet. My heart raced in my chest as I turned toward the sound. The streets were now filled with black smoke, thick and choking, swirling like a living creature that had taken over the city. I could hear the screams, the panic rising as it engulfed everything in its path. People ran in every direction, their faces wide with terror, their eyes filled with confusion and fear.

The stampede began almost immediately. A wave of humanity, desperate to escape, crashed through the streets. Feet pounded the pavement, the sound deafening. Bodies collided, crashing into one another as they fled, the stampede growing more chaotic by the second. It was impossible to move. Everywhere I looked, people were falling, stumbling, tripping, being trampled by those behind them. Their cries for help were drowned out by the chaos around them.

I felt the push of the crowd behind me, shoving me forward, pulling me into the madness. The smell of smoke and sweat mixed with the coppery scent of blood in the air. People were crushed underfoot, their lives stolen in an instant by the mob, their bodies forgotten in the frenzied rush to survive. I could hear the screams, the cries of those unable to escape, but it all felt distant, like a nightmare that I was trapped in.

In the middle of the madness, I realized with horror that it wasn't just the stampede causing the chaos. The mosque, the very place I had tried to avoid, was burning. Flames licked at the sky, reaching higher and higher, as thick black smoke poured from the building, swallowing everything in its path. Someone had set it alight. The holy place that had been full of prayers and peace just hours ago was now a beacon of destruction. The fire raged uncontrollably, fueled by the fear and confusion in the streets below.

I ran. I didn't know where, didn't care. My legs carried me, driven by pure instinct. But the streets were blocked, packed with people fleeing for their lives. There was nowhere to go, nowhere to hide. The heat from the fire was unbearable, even from a distance, and the smoke made it hard to breathe. My throat burned with every breath, my lungs gasping for air that wasn't there.

I stumbled into an alleyway, desperate for a moment of respite, the chaos still echoing in the distance. I pressed myself into the shadows, hidden from the madness around me. The city outside was unrecognizable, consumed by the nightmare that had unfolded in a matter of minutes. I could still hear the screams, the sirens, the sound of emergency vehicles rushing toward the scene. But it was too late. The damage had been done.

From the darkness of my hiding place, I watched as the local police and ambulances arrived, their flashing lights cutting through the smoky haze. News reporters scrambled to capture the disaster, their cameras pointed at the burning mosque, as if they could ever hope to capture the scale of the horror that had just unfolded. But there was no way to explain it. No way to make sense of what had happened. The streets were littered with bodies, their blood staining the ground, while others clung desperately to life, their hands reaching out for help. But there was no help. Not here. Not now.

The mosque, the heart of the community, was gone. Reduced to nothing but charred remains. I couldn't bring myself to imagine the horror within its walls, the people trapped, the lives lost. It was too much. The first day of Ramadan, a time meant for reflection, peace, and spiritual connection, had turned into a blood-soaked nightmare. And I, a stranger in a foreign land, could only watch in horror as the city bled.

The day faded into a thick, suffocating night. The smoke from the fire hung in the air, heavy and acrid, lingering over the city like a permanent stain. The burning of the mosque was just the beginning. In the streets, the aftermath of the attack was still unfolding, people frantically searching for their loved ones, calling out their names in desperation, their voices hoarse with grief and fear. The city was broken, its spirit shattered by the horror that had struck on the first day of Ramadan.

The air was thick with sorrow. Everywhere I looked, people were crying, wailing for those they had lost. But the streets were filled with bodies, some crushed underfoot in the stampede, others burned beyond recognition in the fire. The streets were so congested with the dead that it was impossible to move without stepping over someone's lifeless body. The scene was unreal, as if the world itself had been swallowed by a nightmare that no one could escape.

I wandered through the chaos, the weight of it pressing on my chest, making it hard to breathe. The noise of sirens, the cries of the wounded, and the whispers of shock and disbelief blended into one overwhelming sound. People were still searching for their families, still looking for those who had been lost in the panic. But for many, the search was in vain. The bodies in the streets were all they had left.

I couldn't help but feel the weight of their loss, even though I was a stranger in this land. I wasn't a Muslim; I was just visiting family, caught in the madness of a city that had suddenly turned into a war zone. My family was safe, far from the mosque and the attack. But the image of the burning building, the screams, the blood, it stayed with me. It haunted me, as it would haunt everyone who had witnessed the horror of that day.

Samantha

The next morning, the sun rose, but it felt cold and distant. The streets were quieter now, but the silence was heavy, suffocating. People walked through the ruins, still searching for their loved ones, still reeling from the shock. The bodies had been cleared, the street vendors had returned, and life was slowly beginning to move again. But the trauma of that night was carved into the hearts of everyone who had witnessed it. The wounds would not heal quickly, if at all.

I could still smell the burning mosque, the stench of blood and charred remains. It was like the city itself had been marked, scarred by the violence of the attack. No one could escape it. No one could forget what had happened.

As the days passed, I found myself unable to shake the image of the mosque burning, the faces of the dead, the helplessness in the air. I had never seen anything like it, such a tragedy on the first day of Ramadan, a time meant for peace and reflection. But now, that peace had been replaced by fear and sorrow. The holiday had been stolen by violence, and the wounds would take far longer to heal than the broken bodies on the streets.

Though the city would eventually rebuild, and the lives lost would be mourned, I knew that nothing would ever be the same. The memory of that day, the horror that had unfolded, would linger in the hearts of the survivors, like an unhealed scar. For them, for me, for everyone who had been touched by the terror of that day, Ramadan would never be the same.

Haunting Ghost Train Bleeds

The job was hectic. Some days it felt like my body was made of nothing but exhaustion. Being a tour guide meant a lot of traveling, often by train or on foot, but I didn't mind the plane rides so much. They were a break from the chaos. I've always loved the way the world looks from above, the clouds breaking apart as you descend, the land below dotted with patches of green and brown. It was peaceful, even though everything else in my life felt like it was moving too fast.

But the job wasn't all glamour. Most of the time, I was dragging myself from one tour to another, trying to keep up with the tourists and make sure they had a good experience. There were long days and short days. The heat, the endless walking, it all slowed me down. Still, it was a good gig, most of my expenses were covered. I was lucky, really, to be able to explore different countries, show people the sights, and get paid for it.

This time, though, I was in India. A country of endless life, endless noise, endless crowds. I had a planned train tour through the Indian capital, a sightseeing trip across the villages and landmarks for a group of tourists who were itching to explore. I knew it would be busy, the train would be packed, but it was all part of the experience, right?

The day arrived. I woke up early, the sunlight already slanting through the curtains. I had to get to the station to catch the 7 a.m. train. I booked a taxi and headed out. When I got to the station, the crowds were already gathering. Large groups of people pushed and shoved their way through the gates. I couldn't even imagine how I was going to get a seat, but I figured I'd be lucky if I could even stand for the entire ride.

The carriages were jam-packed with people, like sardines in a tin. The heat was unbearable, thick and suffocating. Sweat clung to my skin, and my clothes stuck to me like they were glued on. I tried not to think about it. There was nothing I could do. The train wasn't going to wait for me to get comfortable, and neither would the people trying to squeeze their way through.

Samantha

I spent several hours on that train, the air so humid that it felt like I was breathing in water. It was uncomfortable, but I couldn't help but laugh to myself. I was just like everyone else, stuck in this cramped space, trying to make it through the day. India, busy and vibrant, had a way of swallowing you whole, and I wasn't the exception.

Finally, after what seemed like an eternity, we entered a dark tunnel. I couldn't see anything outside, and it felt like it went on forever. Time seemed to stretch in that tunnel, and just when I thought it would never end, I felt something strange. Something wet and sticky, as though someone had spilled a drink on me. I looked down at my white shirt and shorts. My clothes, once dry, were now stained. I stared in shock, my shirt turning black, and the spots of red that were now covering me sent a chill down my spine.

I couldn't explain it. It wasn't just a drink. It wasn't rain. It was… blood.

I froze for a moment, staring at the bloodstains on my clothes, unsure of what was happening. My heart started to race as I tried to make sense of it. I'd been sitting still, sweating in the heat, and yet somehow, somehow, my white shirt was covered in what looked like blood. I glanced around, but no one else seemed to notice. No one was reacting to the sudden, disturbing change. The train continued its rattle through the dark tunnel, oblivious to my shock.

I tried to brush it off, figuring it was just some freak accident. Maybe someone spilled something, though I couldn't recall anyone being close enough to me. I even looked around, half expecting to see someone wiping their hands, but there was no one in sight. Just bodies, pressed close together in the sweltering heat, everyone seemingly too tired to care about anything beyond the next station.

But then, a voice.

It came from nowhere, low, soft, and impossibly close. It sent a shiver down my spine, like fingers trailing down the back of my neck. At first, I thought it was my mind playing tricks on me. Maybe it was the heat or the overwhelming discomfort of the situation, but the voice came again, unmistakable this time.

"Kill them," it whispered.

I blinked, my heart thumping painfully in my chest. The voice was distant, yet familiar, like a memory I couldn't quite reach.

"Kill them," it repeated. "Five of them."

I shook my head, trying to clear the fog from my brain. This was insane. I wasn't a murderer. I wasn't about to listen to some ghost telling me to kill people. The thought made my stomach twist, but the voice lingered, creeping in the corners of my mind, soft and insistent.

"Kill them... five of them."

I squeezed my eyes shut, trying to push it away. This wasn't real. It couldn't be. The train was still speeding along, the endless heat pressing in on me. I could feel the sweat running down my back, the uncomfortable weight of the blood on my clothes, but none of it made sense.

Then, another tunnel. Dark. Deeper than the last. It felt like the train was moving through endless blackness, stretching farther than it ever should have. My eyes were heavy, and I realized I was so tired, tired of fighting whatever was taking over. Maybe I was just exhausted. Maybe the heat was getting to me, or maybe I'd lost my mind entirely.

But the voice didn't stop. It kept whispering.

"You must... you must..."

And then, a strange thing happened. As the train sped through the tunnel, I felt myself drift, the world around me slipping away. It wasn't like falling asleep, it was like being pulled into something deeper, something darker. My body felt heavy, numb. I couldn't move, couldn't scream. I was trapped in a fog, floating in and out of consciousness, my thoughts tangled with the voice that had taken over my mind.

Samantha

I didn't know how long it lasted. It could have been seconds, minutes, or hours. When the train finally emerged from the tunnel, I woke with a jolt, my heart hammering in my chest. But the blood, the voice, none of it had disappeared. It was still there, clinging to me like a shadow.

I looked around, my mind reeling. The train was still moving, but something was wrong. The people around me were still standing, still breathing, but there was a strange stillness in the air. No one was talking. No one was laughing or complaining about the heat. It was like the life had drained out of the carriage, leaving only empty bodies moving in a daze.

The smell of blood was thick, filling my nostrils, but it wasn't just the stain on my shirt. It was everywhere now, like it had soaked into the very walls of the train.

And then, as if on cue, I noticed something on the floor, bodies. Slumped, lifeless, their limbs twisted at unnatural angles. I gasped, my breath catching in my throat. How had they gotten there? How had I not seen them before?

I looked down at my hands, my fingers trembling. They were covered in something wet, slick. The invisible knife the ghost had left in my hands. It was there, though I couldn't feel it. It was like I had somehow taken part in the massacre around me without even knowing it. How many people had I... hurt?

The train continued to move, the bodies on the floor a gruesome reminder of what had happened in the darkness. The blood was everywhere now, seeping through the cracks in the floor, staining the walls. It was a nightmare. I didn't know if I was still asleep or if I had truly lost my mind.

But when the train finally slowed to a stop, and the doors opened to reveal the station, I could hardly breathe. I looked around, my heart still racing, my body shaking. No one seemed to notice. The bodies, the blood, it was like it had never existed. People got off the train, laughing, talking, as though nothing was wrong. As though the nightmare I had just lived through was nothing but a dream.

I stumbled off the train, not sure if I was awake or still trapped in the ghost's world, with the invisible knife still clenched in my hands. The air outside was cool, but the weight of what had happened inside that train was unbearable.

I flagged a taxi, trying to escape it all, not knowing if the nightmare had truly ended or if it would follow me.

I barely remember how I got to the hotel. The journey was a blur, like I was walking through a fog that wouldn't lift. I could still feel the blood on my skin, a sticky reminder of the nightmare I couldn't escape. The invisible knife, still hanging in my hands, seemed to pulse with a malevolent energy. I didn't know if I was awake or if I was still trapped in that train, the ghost's whispers echoing in my mind. But when I reached the hotel, I was desperate for something normal. Some piece of reality that could pull me back from the abyss.

I checked in, my hands trembling as I signed the register. The clerk barely looked up. No one seemed to notice the chaos swirling inside me. I was barely holding it together. I didn't trust myself. How could I? I had no idea what had happened on that train, what I had done. The bodies... the blood... it all felt so real, but no one else seemed to see it.

The room was small, bare except for the basics. I sank onto the bed, the weight of my body too much for me to bear. I tried to push the memories away, but they wouldn't go. The blood, the whispering ghost, the bodies that I had somehow missed, lying in plain sight as if they were invisible to everyone but me. I felt trapped, suffocated by the weight of it all.

I closed my eyes, willing myself to sleep. I told myself that when I woke up, it would all be gone. I just needed rest. The kind of deep, peaceful rest that would erase the images of blood and death. But the moment I closed my eyes, sleep didn't come. Instead, the ghost's voice returned.

"You must finish it," it whispered, low and cold, like ice trailing across my spine. "You cannot escape."

I sat up, my heart pounding in my chest. The room felt smaller now, the walls pressing in on me. The air was thick, suffocating. I looked around, but nothing had changed. The same bare walls, the same empty space. But the voice was still there, crawling through my thoughts, dragging me back into the nightmare I thought I had escaped.

I stumbled to the window, desperate for some air, some escape from the prison I had built inside my own mind. But when I looked out, the streets below were empty. The city felt abandoned, like it had been sucked dry of life. I could see the shadows moving between the buildings, but they weren't people. They were something darker, something that shouldn't have been there.

I turned away from the window, my mind spinning. I needed to get out, but where could I go? I had already tried to escape the train, but it had followed me here, lingering in the corners of my mind. The ghost wouldn't leave me. It wanted something from me, something I couldn't understand.

I had to get out.

But as I reached for the door, the room darkened. The lights flickered, and I felt the temperature drop, like the air itself was turning cold and dead. A shadow appeared in the corner of the room, its form shifting, twisting, until it took shape. The ghost, standing in the darkness, watching me.

"You can't hide," it whispered, its voice like a knife cutting through my sanity. "You are mine."

I stumbled back, my chest tightening with panic. The ghost moved closer, its form blurry, like smoke, but I could feel its presence, its coldness wrapping around me. My breath quickened, and I could feel my hands shaking as I clutched at my shirt, desperate to keep myself together.

The door was still there. The only way out. I grabbed the handle, pulling the door open, but the hallway beyond was empty. No escape. No way out. The ghost's whispers grew louder, closer, as if it was right behind me, breathing down my neck.

"You belong to me now," it hissed. "Finish what you started."

I couldn't breathe. I couldn't think. The world felt like it was closing in on me, the walls pressing together, the shadow growing until it swallowed the entire room. My vision blurred, and I could hear my heartbeat, frantic and loud in my ears.

And then, just as suddenly as it had all begun, it stopped. The room went quiet, the air still. I was alone again, but I couldn't shake the feeling that the ghost was still there, waiting, watching.

I looked around the empty hallway. No sign of anyone. No one was watching, no one was there to see what had just happened. The nightmare had shifted again, and I had no idea where I was anymore.

I ran.

I didn't care where I went. I just had to get away from it all. But even as I left the hotel, I knew the ghost would follow me. It had already marked me. There was no escaping what I had seen, what I had done.

And I knew, deep down, that the nightmare wasn't over. It was only just beginning.

River Runs Cold

It was June. The air was warm, the days were long, and summer was in full swing. My friend and I had been talking for weeks about what to do for the summer, tossing around ideas like kids with endless possibilities. After some laughing and joking, we finally settled on an idea that felt just right: a weekend camping trip in the local woods. The idea of getting away from everything, surrounded by nature, seemed perfect. No distractions, no worries, just us, the trees, and the stars.

We started planning, routing out our camping gear and deciding the best time to go. A week from that day felt like the perfect window, summer was in full swing, and we knew the weather would be excellent. The anticipation grew as the days passed, and when the time finally came, we were ready. A night of early sleep was the only thing left before our adventure could begin.

The morning of the trip came, and with it, an excitement that was impossible to ignore. We were up early, barely able to contain our energy as we packed the car with camping supplies. Sleeping bags, tents, food, it all found its place in the trunk. We'd had breakfast, showered, and were ready to head out. I locked up the house, made sure the alarm system was on, and with one last glance around, I hopped into the car.

We were finally off, driving toward the woods with a sense of freedom that only a summer adventure could bring. The excitement buzzed between us as we cruised down the road, our walking boots already on, ready for the journey ahead. We knew the woods could be dangerous, but that only made it feel more thrilling. We felt like explorers, stepping into the unknown.

Arriving at the woods, we parked the car and unloaded our camping gear. The trees loomed overhead, their tall trunks casting shadows over the path. The entrance to the woods was marked by a large metal gate, a kind of barrier to keep out any wild animals that might wander into the area. A small, weathered sign hung by the gate: "Welcome to the

Nature Reserve Woods." It felt official, like we were entering some sacred, untamed land, ready to experience nature in its rawest form.

We walked down a dry, dusty path that wound between the towering trees. The woods were dense, the canopy above thick and almost suffocating, but it didn't scare us. The sun filtered through the leaves, sending sparkling rays down to the forest floor. It was hot, but not unbearable, just the kind of weather that made everything feel alive.

We kept walking, not in a hurry, just taking in the sights and sounds around us. It took us about an hour to find the perfect spot, a small grassy area tucked away from the main trail. The ground was dry, but soft enough for us to set up camp. The heat made it feel still, almost like the woods were holding their breath, waiting for something to happen. But we didn't mind. We were too caught up in the excitement of being out there, away from the usual routines.

Setting up our camp didn't take long. We pitched the tent, laid out the sleeping bags, and arranged our gear. There was no breeze, but the sun was still high, making the air thick with warmth. Once everything was in place, we decided to head out in search of a river. We'd need water, after all, and we figured the river would be the best place to find it.

It was about a 30-minute walk from camp to the river. We walked side by side, the dry path crunching beneath our boots, our steps muffled by the heavy air. As we got closer to the water, we could hear the gentle rush of the current in the distance, a sound that promised relief from the heat. When we finally reached it, we saw the waterfall, a beautiful fountain of rock, the water cascading down in a sparkling spray.

We sat on the bank, our feet in the cool water, letting the river's current wash over us. There wasn't anyone else around, just the two of us and the woods. It felt peaceful, the perfect moment of calm before the evening. We chatted, laughed, and paddled our feet, enjoying the stillness of the moment.

Samantha

But as the sun began to dip lower in the sky, something felt off. That's when I first saw him, the stranger, standing at the edge of the trees, just watching us.

At first, we thought nothing of it. Just some guy out for a walk, maybe another camper passing through. But the longer we stared, the more unsettling it became. He stood there, motionless, barely visible between the dense trees. His figure was tall, too tall, and he didn't move a muscle. I felt a twinge of unease crawling up my spine, but I tried to shake it off.

We went back to paddling our feet in the cool water, trying to enjoy the quiet moment, but the stranger was still there, unmoving. He hadn't taken a single step forward or back, just watched us. The light from the setting sun cast strange shadows through the trees, making his figure look more like a part of the woods than a person.

"I don't like the look of him," my friend murmured, glancing over at the stranger. His voice was low, but the tension in it was clear. "What do you think he's doing?"

I shrugged, though my own stomach had tightened. "Maybe he's just passing through. Probably just a hiker or something."

But deep down, I knew something wasn't right. The way he stood there, the way his eyes never seemed to blink, it made the hairs on the back of my neck stand up.

We tried to ignore him, but the sky was growing darker, and the air around us felt heavy. It was almost as if the world itself was holding its breath. The stranger was still there. His eyes never left us, and I could feel them like a weight on my skin.

The sun was setting, painting the sky with hues of orange and pink, and the world around us felt like it was shifting into something else, something darker. We decided it was time to head back to camp. The sun had almost disappeared beyond the horizon, and the woods were growing colder.

151

But as we stood up to leave, my friend's eyes darted to the stranger once more.

"Hey, he's still there," my friend said, a mix of confusion and fear in their voice.

I turned to look, my pulse quickening. The stranger had moved. Slowly, like he was gliding across the earth, he stepped into the shadows, but I could still see him, his face now clearer, his mask… no, it wasn't a mask. It was a face, too pale, too still. A human face, but twisted, hollowed-out, with eyes that were too wide. It was like a dead man's face, frozen in some grim expression.

Suddenly, the man started moving again, but this time he wasn't walking casually. He was charging, running fast, a wild speed I couldn't comprehend. The machete he carried swung wildly above his head, catching the last glimmers of light before it was swallowed by the shadows.

My heart froze. "Run!" I shouted, grabbing my friend's arm.

We bolted, our feet pounding the earth as we rushed toward the woods' edge. But he was fast, too fast. He closed the distance between us in seconds, his figure shifting through the trees like a nightmare brought to life.

"Run, just run!" I screamed again, not daring to look back, knowing he was right behind us.

We reached the water's edge, gasping for breath, but the stranger wasn't far behind. He was now only a few feet away, waving the machete as if he meant to slice us down where we stood. His presence was suffocating, like a force that wouldn't let us escape.

And then, as if in some horrifying twist, I saw something else, body parts, floating up from the river's dark depths. At first, it was just one hand, pale and lifeless, followed by a foot, an arm, a leg. They bobbed to the surface as though the river had been hiding them, waiting for us to see. My stomach lurched, and I couldn't breathe. The water was tainted, cursed in some unimaginable way.

Samantha

"Get the knife!" I gasped, feeling like the air had been sucked out of my lungs.

My friend scrambled through their bag, finally pulling out a kitchen knife. But the stranger didn't slow down. The machete sliced the air as he lunged at us. His movements were terrifyingly quick, like an animal in a frenzy. My friend stabbed the knife into his side, but it barely slowed him down. The stranger just kept coming, his face expressionless, the human mask locked in a deathly stare.

Then, with one final swing, the machete grazed my forehead. Pain shot through my skull, and I staggered back, but we didn't stop. We couldn't stop.

The last thing I remember before everything went blank was the stranger's blood-soaked apron and the sound of the river, cold and cruel.

I woke up with a start, my head pounding, my forehead burning where the machete had struck me. The world around me was a blur, and for a moment, I wasn't sure where I was. My legs felt like they were made of lead, and the cold, damp feeling of the river water still clung to my skin.

But there was no time to gather my thoughts. The stranger, **that thing**, was still out there, and we were in no state to fight anymore. I glanced over at my friend. They were shaky, bloodied but alive. I felt a sharp pang of relief. We were still together, still breathing.

The river, once a place of peaceful respite, now felt like a tomb. The sight of those body parts floating, the dead hands and limbs, made my stomach churn. I couldn't shake the feeling that something dark had been watching us all along. We had wandered into a nightmare, and now there was no escape.

"Come on," I whispered hoarsely, my voice barely more than a rasp. "We need to go. Now."

We stumbled toward the woods' edge, our steps sluggish and weak. The sun had dipped below the horizon, leaving the woods in a shadowy, suffocating twilight. The forest seemed to close in on us, the trees bending and shifting in the wind, like they were alive, watching. We couldn't hear anything except the sounds of our ragged breaths and the eerie rustle of the leaves.

Then, a sound, a slithering, hissing sound, came from behind us.

I froze.

A snake, large, coiled, its body rippling through the underbrush. Its scales glinted in the dim light, its tongue flicking in and out. Its eyes locked onto us, cold and calculating, like it was stalking its prey. My blood ran cold. We weren't just fighting against the woods and the stranger anymore. Now, we had to face a creature that didn't care whether we were human or not.

It was a deadly, venomous snake, its body long and thick, the kind of snake that didn't hesitate to strike. We had no weapons left. No machete. No knife. Just the two of us, barely standing, trying to make it out of this nightmare.

"Don't move," I whispered, my voice trembling. "Just stay still. It might leave."

But the snake didn't leave. It was too close now. It raised its head, its mouth opening to reveal fangs that looked sharp enough to tear through bone. I could feel its venomous presence, the death that radiated off of it, creeping closer with every second.

We had no choice. We couldn't just stand there and wait. We needed to get out, to run, but the snake had cornered us. It was watching us, its movements slow and deliberate. The tension in the air was unbearable.

I felt like my heart was going to explode in my chest. I couldn't think. I couldn't breathe.

And then, in a flash, the snake lunged.

We jumped to the side, barely avoiding its strike. The air around us was thick with panic as we scrambled, not caring about anything except survival. We ran, not looking back, not daring to see if the snake was following us. My legs burned with every step, but we kept moving. We ran until the world around us was just a blur of trees and shadows.

Somehow, we found the edge of the woods, the parking lot just beyond the trees. My hands were shaking as I fumbled for the car keys. The panic was so intense I could barely focus, but somehow I got the door open. My friend dove into the car, slamming the door shut behind them. I was right behind them, my body screaming in pain, but the car was a sanctuary. The snake wasn't following us. Not anymore.

The engine roared to life, and I floored the gas pedal. We sped away, the woods disappearing behind us, but I could still feel the weight of it all pressing down on me. The terror, the horror of what we had just experienced, it hadn't disappeared with the snake. It was still in the car with us, suffocating us in the silence that filled the space between us.

We drove without saying a word, both of us lost in our own thoughts, our minds replaying every horrifying moment. The stranger, the body parts, the snake. It was all one never-ending nightmare, and I couldn't shake the feeling that it wasn't over yet.

It would never be over. The woods had changed us. The things we had seen in that place weren't just figments of our imagination, they were real. And the fear they had instilled in us would never fade.

I glanced at my friend, their eyes wide with the same terror that I could feel twisting in my gut.

"Never again," I said quietly, the words slipping from my mouth before I could stop them. "We're never going back to those woods."

They nodded, but I knew the truth. We wouldn't have to. The woods would come for us, in our dreams, in our thoughts, in the shadows. We had escaped the nightmare, but it had followed us.

We survived. But the woods, they would never let us forget.

The Rainbow Crys

The sun was dazzling, too dazzling, burning its golden weight across the earth like it meant to scorch something clean. The sky above me was bare, not a single cloud in sight, just a crystal sheet of blue stretched from horizon to horizon. The kind of sky that feels endless, the kind that dares you to look too long.

I was outside in my garden. The soil was dry, but it held a kind of warmth that made it easy to dig through, and I had decided it was the perfect day for rose planting. There was so much to do. So much to prepare. I wanted everything to look just right for summer, I always did.

I got to work, tugging up the turf with both hands, the earth splitting apart with a soft, satisfying tear. I made small holes for the seeds, neat and clean, like little graves for beauty to grow from. The sun soaked through my skin, heat rising off the garden floor in invisible waves. It took most of the day, and yet, time didn't feel like it moved at all. Just the rhythm of soil and sweat, and the occasional whisper of a breeze that never stayed long enough to matter.

When lunchtime arrived, I didn't bother going inside. I made myself a plate and sat right there in the garden, cross-legged on the patio, eating slowly and watching the world go by. I had an egg sandwich in one hand and a little bowl of strawberry ice cream in the other, two waffers tucked in, softening as the cold melted beneath the heat. It felt like a small treat, a quiet reward.

I stared up at the sky, still impossibly blue, and my thoughts drifted, somewhere between the stillness of the garden and the shimmer of the air. I started thinking about a rainbow. Not just any rainbow, but one made of magic colours, too vivid to be real, the kind of thing you don't expect to see but always hope to. It was strange, how deeply I began to imagine it. A rainbow with meaning. A rainbow with a secret.

I let the thought stay with me for a while. I took my time eating. Let the sun bake against my arms. Tried to cool myself down with each bite of melting strawberry.

Then, when the food was gone and the stillness settled again, I got back to work.

I returned to the flower beds, hands buried in the warm earth. The rest of the planting took a few hours more. I covered each small hole with care, pressing the dirt down gently, like sealing something precious away.

I didn't know then what was coming.

I didn't know how fast beauty could turn.

It happened quickly.

One moment, I was smoothing over the final patch of earth, hands caked in soil, breath steady beneath the weight of the sun. The next, the sky began to change.

A sudden overcast swept across the blue like a curtain drawn too fast. Shadows crawled over the garden beds. I looked up, squinting. The sky was no longer endless, it had become a rushing grey, folding over itself with a strange urgency.

I dropped everything and rushed to the rose bed. My fingers fumbled to cover the freshly planted soil, pressing in the corners, patting the top to hold it in place. The wind began to blow, sharp, erratic, lifting strands of my hair and tugging at my clothes like it wanted to drag me inside.

Then came the rain.

First a spot. A single, cold drop against my skin.

Then more. All at once.

The sky burst open like it had been waiting to pour itself out. The clouds turned heavy and bruised, and the downpour came down in sheets. I had no time to grab anything. My garden tools were left behind, abandoned in the grass. I ran into the house, the rain soaking my back before I'd even reached the door.

Inside, everything felt quieter than it should have. I shut the door behind me, heart still beating fast. I turned to the window and watched.

The storm pressed up against the glass like a living thing. Rain hit the panes with hard, slanted streaks. Then a sudden crack, lightning, jagged and too close, lit up the garden in a blinding white flash. I jumped, pulling the curtains closed in one motion.

Thunder followed like a growl.

I sat down, trying to breathe through the heaviness. My hands were shaking a little, not from fear exactly, but from the suddenness of it all. Then came the sound of hail, sharp and violent, like fists slamming into the windows. They bounced off like stones, no, like golf balls, each impact rattling the glass in its frame.

The ground outside was drowned. The garden transformed into a pool of mud and movement. I couldn't see my tools anymore.

I made myself a cup of tea. Just something warm to hold. I wasn't even hungry, but I reached for a biscuit anyway. It felt like the right thing to do, something normal in the middle of what wasn't.

Outside, it was black.

Not night. Not evening. Just black.

The kind of black that doesn't have edges. I didn't even dare switch on the TV, it didn't feel safe. The lightning was still out there, pulsing through the air like a warning.

The hours passed slowly, and still I sat there, listening.

Waiting.

Eventually, I noticed the thunder was fading. The hail had stopped. I no longer felt the house shake with every flash. A stillness returned, hesitant and strange. I didn't trust it.

But I stood anyway.

I walked to the window and peeked through the curtain. It was lighter, not bright, but no longer suffocating. I opened the door. Just a crack.

The air smelled like wet earth and electricity. The garden was drenched, water pooling around the plants and soaking deep into the soil. I slipped on my waterproof shoes, the kind I kept for mornings heavy with dew, and stepped outside.

The ground squished beneath me, thick and soft, like the garden had turned to sponge. But the roses… the storm had done something good for them. The beds were soaked through. I wouldn't have to water a thing.

Still, the sky was restless. The clouds hovered above in heavy grey waves, refusing to leave.

And then I saw it.

An arch. Faint at first, rising slowly out of the misted light.

A rainbow.

But it wasn't beautiful.

Not yet.

It was still raining, not heavy now, but soft, strange droplets, falling from a sky that had already emptied itself. The storm had ended. I could feel it. Yet the rain… it lingered. Almost like it didn't want to go.

I looked up again at the rainbow.

It had taken full shape now, a perfect arch stretched across the sky. Its colours were vivid, almost too vivid, bleeding into one another like wet paint. It should've been beautiful.

But it wasn't.

Because it was making a sound.

At first I thought it was the wind, or maybe something carried over from the storm. But no, it was coming from the rainbow itself. A low, distant noise. Almost like… crying. A weeping sound, thin and shuddering, hanging just above the breeze.

I stared harder.

Rainbows don't cry. They shine. They fade. They don't make noise. They don't… mourn.

Something about it made my skin crawl.

It hung there, upside down at first, like a frown stretched across the sky. The colours felt duller now, warped. I stood frozen in the garden, water soaking through my sleeves. My breath caught as the arch began to shift, curling slowly… flipping… until it turned upright.

Into a smile.

But not a joyful one.

It grinned.

Not metaphorically, it grinned. The arc of it pulled unnaturally high, like a mouth with no face. Then came the glint, sharp, gleaming points tucked within the colours.

Teeth.

Hidden teeth.

I blinked once, hard. My mind reeled. No, no, it couldn't be. Rainbows don't have teeth. Rainbows don't watch you.

But it was watching me.

I couldn't see the eyes, but I felt them. Somewhere, just behind the shimmer, behind the colour, there were eyes. Invisible, but real. Unblinking. Fixed on me.

Then, laughter.

Low at first, then rising, echoing in the air above my garden. Not a laugh of joy. Not light. Not human. It was wrong. Twisted. Something cruel hiding in a sound meant to be innocent.

I felt a drop land on my face.

Another.

I looked up.

It wasn't rain. It wasn't even water. Just… wet. Cold. Strange. The storm was long over. There was no reason for it now, nothing left in the clouds to fall.

But still it dripped.

And still the rainbow smiled.

I felt the shivers roll across my skin, rising up my spine. My hair stood on end, pulled by something unseen. I backed away slowly toward the house. My feet sank into the soaked ground. The laughter hadn't stopped.

It got louder.

I told myself it couldn't hurt me.

It was a rainbow. A sky thing. It couldn't move, couldn't touch. It didn't have legs. It didn't have hands.

But it had a mouth. And it had a voice.

And something, someone, must have cursed it.

Because this was no ordinary light and rain illusion. This was no child's fantasy arched across the sky. It was something darker. Something sent. Something alive.

I slammed the door behind me, breath ragged. Curtains drawn tight.

Eventually, the sky began to clear. The rainbow faded, slow and thin, disappearing into blue. But I never forgot.

Even now, the image still haunts me, that wicked grin in the sky, those invisible eyes, the way it laughed.

The roses will bloom, I'm sure. The rain did them good. My garden will be beautiful.

But I never want to see another rainbow again.

Not like that one.

Not ever.

The Devils Sand

It was a scorching day. The kind of heat that presses down on you from above and rises up from the ground all at once , a desert sun, merciless and wide-eyed. We had just landed. An adventure holiday, my friend had said. He wanted to ride a camel. Said it was on his list. Something about the stillness of the sand, the sway of the dunes. I wasn't convinced, but I went anyway.

The morning had already been long. Airports blur together , check-ins, queues, suitcases groaning on conveyor belts. I barely remembered boarding. But now the plane was parked at the terminal, the engine winding down with a sigh. The captain made his final announcement as people unbuckled, stood, stretched.

The flight had been quiet, uneventful. But the second the cabin door opened, the heat struck like a wall , dry and full of weight. We stepped out onto the tarmac, blinking against the sunlight. It dazzled, pouring down like molten glass over the palm trees and the cracking earth. The sky was painfully blue , cloudless, endless, too perfect.

We found our suitcases spinning slowly on the belt and grabbed them, wheeling them outside in the direction of waiting taxis. The air shimmered. Even the wind carried heat in it.

When we reached our hotel, I stopped in my tracks.

It looked... wrong.

Not wrong in an obvious way , no broken windows or caution tape. But something in the bones of the place made my stomach tighten. It wasn't five-star, not even close. More like one-star dressed up in fake promises. The walls were sun-bleached and tired. The entrance gave nothing away. A few other holiday-goers lingered around the entrance, some looking just as confused.

We checked in. The receptionist barely made eye contact. We took our room keys and unlocked the door with cautious hands.

Inside wasn't terrible.

Clean sheets. A kettle. Tea, coffee, a few sachets of sugar tossed on a tray. The TV hummed with static before clicking to life , voices speaking in a language we didn't understand. Music buzzed softly through the hallway from somewhere unseen.

We decided to rest. Jet lag was a whisper at the back of my skull. We needed the sleep , tomorrow was our desert tour. But after a while, we woke, restless, pulled by curiosity. We wanted to stretch our legs, feel something of the place beyond the walls of the room.

The streets outside were narrow and winding, lined with old shops and market stalls. Everything looked aged , beautifully so. Doors carved with forgotten symbols. Stone paths worn smooth by years of footsteps. The air was still hot, but less sharp now , the sun lowering behind the buildings.

We ate at a small place tucked between two alleys. A Moroccan feast , rich spices, soft bread, dishes that filled the table. It was cheap, too. Cheaper than it should've been.

Later, we drifted to the square, drawn by the music. Snake charmers played their flutes, swaying with their rhythm, coaxing movement from the ground. Cobras slithered and rose on cue, big and glossy under the streetlamps. A man approached, offering to take our photo beside them. We said no. Something about it felt... wrong. Performative. Off. He didn't press.

We stayed there for a little while, watching, not speaking much.

Then we went back to the hotel. The room was still quiet. The sheets still clean.

Tomorrow was the desert.

We didn't know it yet , but something was already waiting for us in the dunes.

The morning arrived fast, pulling us out of sleep before the sun had properly risen. Our alarms buzzed through the quiet. We moved like shadows , shower, clothes, a rushed breakfast in a dining hall too quiet for comfort. The hotel lobby felt different this time, like the walls were watching. Maybe it was the early hour. Maybe it was something else.

The tour guide was waiting. A few other guests stood nearby, yawning, adjusting scarves and backpacks. We boarded the bus, its engine grumbling in the early heat. The city fell away behind us. Concrete gave way to stone. Then to sand.

And then, nothing but dunes.

Endless dunes.

The desert opened up like another world , all curve and glare and wind. It moved, even when it looked still. The sand blew fast across the hills, soft waves under a pale, scorching sky. The wind tugged at our faces. Our feet sank into the ground like it wanted to swallow us whole.

We had sandals on. Our mouths and noses were covered , scarves wrapped tight, trying to keep the sand out. Still, it got in. It always got in.

We walked for a while, rolling down the slopes like children, laughing into the wind. It felt good , light, if only for a moment. There was something about the desert that stripped sound away. Everything was quieter there. Like the land held its breath.

Then came the camel ride.

They brought them out slowly , big, lean creatures, hissing and clicking their teeth. They smelled of heat and dust. My friend grinned like a kid, finally getting his wish. We climbed onto their backs and moved in a long, swaying line , dipping through dunes, the sun burning above, the world around us slowly vanishing into gold.

That's when it changed.

The light first.

It dulled.

Not like a sunset, not natural. Just… dim. The air turned heavy, and without warning, the mist arrived.

Thick. Grey. Swallowing everything.

One by one, the people ahead of us disappeared into the fog. I couldn't see more than a few feet in front of me. Even the camel beneath me felt distant, like we were floating through it. Voices turned to echoes. Then to nothing.

I called out.

No one answered.

Then… I saw something.

A shape in the haze.

A face.

It flickered just beyond the veil , massive, shifting, horned. Eyes that gleamed red through the fog. A mouth stretched wide in something far worse than a grin. My breath caught in my throat.

It looked like a devil.

And it wasn't hiding. It wanted to be seen.

The desert, I realised, was cursed. Touched by something old and angry and waiting. This wasn't just mist. It was something alive. And it was watching us.

Then came the snakes.

Slithering up from beneath the sand. Not one. Not two. Dozens. Their bodies cut paths through the dunes, rattling, fast. The camels shrieked, trying to turn, hissed in protest. Panic bloomed around us like wildfire.

The tour guide yelled something, muffled through the mist. I couldn't hear. I couldn't move.

The devil face rose higher in the fog, towering above the dunes, and laughed. A sound that broke through the sand, the mist, the very air around us. It wasn't human. It didn't need to be.

We turned back.

Samantha

The guide forced the group to retreat, shouting orders, calling names. The camels resisted, then obeyed. Slowly, we moved, half-blinded, stumbling across the shifting hills. Every step felt longer than the last. The snakes followed, their bodies cutting lines behind us.

The devil's laughter never stopped.

It echoed through the dunes like thunder made of teeth.

We didn't speak. We didn't scream. There was no room for sound , only fear.

The mist never lifted.

It just followed us all the way back.

We made it back.

Not quickly. The mist clung to everything, slowing us down, stretching the journey into something dreamlike and cruel. No one spoke on the way. Not really. Just glances. Just silence. The snakes had faded behind us, but I could still feel them. Hear them in the sand. The devil's laughter echoed in my ears long after the sound had stopped.

We waited at the pickup point, standing in a line that felt like a procession. The heat had returned, but not in the same way. It felt sharper now. More personal.

The bus was late.

Only five minutes, maybe less , but it was enough. Enough time to let the fear settle deeper in our bones. We stood still. Listening. Watching. Hoping nothing would rise from the dunes again.

When the bus finally arrived, we boarded without a word.

The ride back was a blur. Sand still in my shoes. Mist still in my throat. The desert didn't let you leave clean. It marked you. Somehow, we'd all made it out. But none of us felt whole.

We reached the hotel just before dusk. The sun had shifted, casting strange angles across the walls. The lobby, once dull and faded, now looked almost warped in the dimming light.

Fear The Bloody Forest In The Dark

Then we saw it.

Chaos.

People running. Screaming. The air thick with panic. A shooting , someone shouted. It was happening inside the hotel. The place we thought we were returning to for safety.

Sirens wailed in the distance, still too far away.

For a moment, it didn't feel real. It felt like we had brought something back with us. Like the devil hadn't stayed in the dunes after all. Like the curse had followed us home.

I stood frozen, suitcase still in hand, watching as someone was pulled away by another guest. I don't remember moving. I don't remember what I said. I only remember the feeling:

That nowhere was safe.

Not the desert.

Not the hotel.

Not even the sky.

Our holiday had been promised as adventure. But what we got was something else entirely. We were hunted by mist, by snakes, by a devil in the dunes. And then, when we thought it was over , we returned to a place where bullets replaced sand, and blood replaced sweat.

We survived it.

But I don't think we ever truly left that desert.

It followed us back.

And I will never go there again.

Not to that place.

Not to the devil's sand.

Samantha

Phantom Of the Theatre

The city glowed with its usual night-time blaze , a thousand lights flickering in windows, headlights streaking down wet streets, neon signs buzzing faintly against the black. It was a typical evening for most. Clubs pulsed in the distance, laughter spilled from open bars, but we weren't here for that.

No booze. No loud music. No clubs.

Just something different.

Me and my three friends had planned this night a week ago , a trip to the local theatre. We wanted something out of the ordinary. A bit of culture, maybe. Something slow, mysterious, atmospheric. We didn't know yet how much of that we'd get , and more.

The theatre loomed ahead of us, dark bricks and golden lights curling around its old face. A crowd had already formed. Long queues snaked from the entrance, people shifting on their feet, checking the time. A few were dressed up , cloaks, masks, face paint. Some of the costumes looked spooky enough to belong to the stage itself. We stood out in our jeans and tops, soft shoes tapping against the concrete.

7:30 PM. The ticket office finally opened.

A sudden rush. Tickets were being snatched up, hands pushing forward, people eager to get the best seats. The air buzzed with impatience. Excitement, maybe. We waited our turn, got our tickets, and slipped into the building's shadows.

Before heading to our seats, we stopped at the bathrooms to freshen up , just a bit of powder, a check in the mirror. The walls in there were old, too. Cracked in places. The lights flickered slightly, but not enough to notice unless you were paying attention.

And I was.

Because for a moment, I felt it.

That crawling sense. Like eyes were fixed on me , not from the mirror, not from the stall next door. But from **somewhere else**. Behind the walls. Inside them.

I turned around fast. Nothing.

Just cold air and cracked tiles.

I brushed it off. Told myself not to be silly. Just nerves. Just atmosphere.

We left the bathroom and found our seats , middle section, clear view of the screen. The theatre was filling up fast now, a soft hum of voices rising beneath the domed ceiling. Then the lights dimmed.

People went quiet.

The curtains pulled back.

And that was when the music started.

Not your usual overture. This was different. The sound was sharp, off-key , like a lullaby gone wrong. Devilish, almost. It twisted up from the speakers like smoke, wrapping around the room, finding its way under your skin. I could see it in the audience. People shifting in their chairs, whispering. Some laughed nervously. Others didn't.

The music dragged on too long. Just long enough to make you question why it hadn't stopped yet.

Then it did.

The screen flickered to life.

The opening scene: a graveyard, mist curling thick between the tombstones. Everything was grey and grainy. Something moved , slow, subtle , beneath the dirt on one of the graves. I leaned in.

A skeleton hand rose up through the soil.

Gasps echoed from the crowd. A few people laughed, but it wasn't real laughter. It was the kind people use to keep fear at bay.

We stayed calm. It was just a film. Just a creepy old show.

Until he appeared.

A figure stepped forward on the screen , tall, dressed in black, thin as bone. Long grey hair spilling out from under a black hat. His hands were enormous, fingers curled unnaturally long. He moved slowly, like he was gliding across the ground.

Then he spoke.

The voice wasn't right. It wasn't distorted, wasn't deep. It was just… wrong. Too dry, too cold, too real. Like it hadn't been recorded. Like it was coming from somewhere else.

Somewhere closer.

The room had gone completely silent.

And for the first time, I wondered if this was still just part of the show.

The phantom on the screen moved slowly, deliberately, his eyes hidden in shadow, his lips curling into something that wasn't quite a smile , but wasn't neutral either. He stared out through the mist like he could see us.

And maybe he could.

The eerie music had returned , but softer this time. It slid beneath the seats, clung to the walls, settled into the spaces between breaths. It felt like it was coming from all directions at once. It didn't rise like a soundtrack. It crept. And I could feel the crowd shift again, whispering, shuffling, like they could all sense something wasn't right but no one wanted to admit it.

I leaned back in my seat, trying to relax.

That's when I felt it.

A hand.

Not a brush. Not a breeze. A hand, grazing across my back , slow, too slow, too real.

I twisted around.

And there he was.

Fear The Bloody Forest In The Dark

Not on the screen anymore.

Standing behind me.

The phantom.

His eyes had turned green, glowing in the dark like something from a nightmare. His skin was pale, waxy, stretched tight across his bones. And when he opened his mouth , his fangs gleamed. Long. Sharp. Wet.

I couldn't move.

He didn't blink. He didn't speak. Just stood there, staring at me with this low, pulsing rage beneath the surface.

This wasn't theatre. This wasn't acting.

This was real.

I grabbed my friend's arm. She turned. Her eyes went wide.

Then came the first scream , not from us, but from somewhere in the front rows. People were rising from their seats, turning, gasping, panicking. And then, from the corners of the theatre , from the balconies, from the shadows , they came.

More of them.

Not just one phantom. Many.

Flying demons, tearing through the air, their eyes burning green and red. Their mouths were wide open, teeth gnashing, blood already dripping from their lips. Some were crawling along the ceiling like spiders, others diving into the crowd.

Chaos exploded.

People screamed and scattered, chairs clattering, shoes pounding down the aisles. The demons descended like a swarm. One of them landed near the stage , its hands hooked like claws , and lunged at a man trying to escape. The sound that followed was something I'll never forget.

Tearing.

Ripping.

Guts hitting the ground.

It wasn't special effects. It wasn't fake blood or clever props. It was real.

The floor was slick. The walls shook. The entire theatre was alive with screaming and slaughter.

And all I could think about was that moment in the bathroom. That shadow I felt watching me. That chill on my neck. I'd brushed it off like nerves.

But it wasn't.

It was them. They had already been there. Already waiting.

The theatre had become unrecognisable.

There was no stage now. No screen. Just blood and bodies. Seats overturned, the carpet soaked in red. Screams had turned to sobbing, to silence, to sounds I'll never forget. The smell of metal and burnt air filled my lungs. Every breath felt like glass.

The phantom was still moving through the chaos , the original one, the one who touched me. He didn't rush. He didn't need to. He walked like the king of it all, like the carnage belonged to him.

Because it did.

This wasn't a haunted theatre.

This was his theatre.

A place built not for stories , but for slaughter.

People tried to run. Some escaped, stumbling into the street, still screaming. But not all of them made it. The demons were fast. Some of them flew. Some of them crawled across the walls, snatching at hair, at skin, at anything soft and moving. Their mouths opened wider than they should have. Their teeth were black with blood. Some were laughing.

I didn't move. I couldn't.

Fear The Bloody Forest In The Dark

I was still in the middle section, crouched low, arms over my head. I felt something wet drip beside me , not water. Not rain.

Blood.

It slid down the side of a seat, warm and slick. Someone above me had been torn open.

And still, the music played.

That same eerie melody from the start, rising up again like a cruel joke. It echoed off the walls, off the bones. It didn't stop , not even when the screaming did. Not even when there was no one left standing near the stage.

I thought of that moment in the bathroom again , how I felt watched, how I ignored it. It hadn't been imagination. It had been the **beginning**. A warning I never listened to.

This phantom wasn't just a shadow behind a mask. He wasn't a character or a ghost. He was something far older. Something demonic. Cold. Bloodthirsty. And this theatre wasn't a venue. It was his feeding ground.

What we thought was a show was a trap. The screen had never been fake. The graveyard, the mist , all of it was real. Somehow broadcast, somehow blended into the theatre itself. A portal, maybe. Or a trick.

People had come for entertainment.

What they got was a butcher's stage.

And though some of us escaped , not many did.

Those who stayed died by a demon's fangs. Torn apart in front of friends. Family. Strangers. The phantom didn't care who you were. Only that you were there.

As I stumbled through the back exit, pushing past what remained of the heavy theatre doors, I looked back once.

The music still played.

The curtains had fallen.

Samantha

And beneath that black, rotting roof…

there was no more audience.

Just bodies.

And a stage soaked in blood.